The S

The Story of a Nobody

Anton Chekhov

Translated by Hugh Aplin

ET REMOTISSIMA PROPE

100 PAGES

100 PAGES

Published by Hesperus Press Limited
4 Rickett Street, London sw6 1ru
www.hesperuspress.com

First published by Hesperus Press Limited, 2002

English language translation and introduction © Hugh Aplin, 2002
Foreword © Louis de Bernières, 2002

Designed and typeset by Fraser Muggeridge
Printed in the United Arab Emirates by Oriental Press

isbn: 1-84391-003-9

CONTENTS

FOREWORD

I came to this story in a state of innocence, inasmuch as, like most of us, I suspect, I was familiar with Chekhov's plays, but not with his prose narratives. Chekhov himself, however, thought of himself as a dramatist only thirdly, and often declared that he was going to give up writing for the theatre altogether, his darkest moment probably being when *The Seagull* was received with absolute hostility on its first night. He was a doctor first, and a prose writer second. He once said that, 'Medicine is my legal spouse, whilst literature is my mistress. When I get tired of one, I go and sleep with the other.' Dramaturgy was presumably an occasional adultery behind the backs of both of them.

Having read *The Story of a Nobody*, I am resolved to read the rest of his tales as soon as I can get hold of them. This one leaves a strange taste in the mouth, to be sure. One finds oneself thinking about it for days afterwards, and it is interesting to try to work out why this is. I have come to my own conclusions, naturally, but something ought to hinder me from revealing them; namely, that it would simply not be Chekhovian, for Chekhov was not interested in telling us what to think. His characters are marvellously observed and wittily portrayed, but he does not indicate which ones we are supposed to admire or disagree with. Everyone has faults and virtues, strength and feebleness. Everyone has a philosophy which is more or less plausible, and we are presented with people in such a way that we find something to understand in all of them. I suspect that this makes Chekhov a more modern writer than virtually everyone who has come afterwards. Being a writer myself probably makes me a peculiar reader, but I have experienced the distinct feeling that I have just picked up a marvellous practical tip.

I was reminded in the first place of Mikhail Yurevich Lermontov's *A Hero of Our Time* (1840), whose protagonist makes a religion of boredom, but I was more struck by the resonance of this story with some of the literature of existentialism. We find a sort of pessimism that is relativistic about human values, we find the idea that all of us are defeated by our own projects, which is what makes us simultaneously tragic, absurd and lovable. People wrestle half-heartedly with the futility of their own lives, not even quite wanting to win, since this entails battles that are really too much effort to engage in. There is the idea, too, that we are essentially superfluous, that we are actors in a world where there are no playwrights, no directors, and theatres only in inaccessible places, where we will inevitably find minute and attentive audiences. We are left improvising distractedly, unable to discern our own destinies, unconvinced by our own performances, but hoping that we will be seen by other people as better or more exciting than we know we really are. Unfortunately, however, hell is precisely those other people. Some of us, like the existentialists, find all this infuriating, some of us no doubt find it sad, but I would suggest that Chekhov doesn't really find it anything at all. He merely invites us to observe it with natural curiosity, and we are free to find it discouraging or funny by turns.

Similarly, we are free to choose our own hero. The only character who is almost entirely unsympathetic is the kleptomaniac maid, Polya, although even she has the redeeming feature of having the blunt impertinence to stick up for herself. One of Orlov's wastrel friends, Gruzin, turns out to be a wise adviser and a soulful pianist. Another, Kukushkin, who cultivates the image of a womaniser, cannot bring himself to become one in fact. We are really presented with a choice of three heroes: Zinaida, the narrator, and Orlov. One can perceive Zinaida as a wronged and tragic figure or as a silly romantic who has got the wrong end of the stick, and who finally treats the narrator almost as cruelly as she herself was treated. The anonymous narrator himself is a tired and sick terrorist who has taken up employment as a servant in the hope of being able to assassinate his employer's important father, which he entirely fails to get around to doing, despite being presented with the ideal opportunity. His own sympathy is entirely with Zinaida, even though she treats him with indifference and he cannot credit how much money she wastes when so much of the world is in poverty. Really, we think, he must be in love with her, even though he denies it. He lives for Zinaida and makes considerable sacrifices for her, because she mysteriously represents for him his dream of the normal life that he can never have, with a house, a garden and children, and a proper job. Ideally he doesn't want Zinaida, but someone just like her, and one wonders whether his affections would always be thus deferred and displaced. The most interesting of his traits is his absolute disgust with the irony and cynicism of everyone around him. As he progressively allows his own ideals to lapse, he grows appalled by the lack of them in everybody else. Perhaps he is drawn to Zinaida in the first place because she is the only one with elevated conceptions of life, even though these are commonplace romantic ones that life will quickly force her to discard, replacing them with ones that the narrator himself is in the process of abandoning.

For my money Orlov is the most interesting character, because his self-knowledge is absolute. He has no illusions about himself at all, and is perplexed and embarrassed by

Zinaida's idolatry. He does have ideals, but he knows that he wouldn't be able to sustain the inconvenience of pursuing them. He despises all classes of men, but would rather be in his own class than any other. He knows his job is a waste of his life, but he quite enjoys the manner of its wasting. He knows that he is intelligent and talented enough to achieve a great deal, but he happily spends all his spare time reading unsystematically, and playing cards. He knows that he just wants a mistress with whom he can have fun when they are both on top form, and he knows that he couldn't be bothered with the proper relationship that he is conventionally supposed to want. He is normally brutally honest, and it is only cowardice that prevents him from telling Zinaida the truth, since her tears undo him utterly, and no discussion can get beyond them. He is frequently cruel to her, because she has put him in a position that he did not expect and does not know how to deal with. At one point he cheerfully agrees with the narrator's damning critique of him, and does the minimally decent thing with respect to his illegitimate daughter. 'How essentially foul it all is!' he exclaims, without any apparent pain. He seems to have achieved the imperturbable indifference of an eastern monk.

Chekhov's lack of an authorial moral stance is one of the things that makes this story both disturbing and entertaining. Although Chekhov's style is curiously transparent, one cannot but be struck by the oddity or profundity of some of the things that he says; 'In Russia, even a noble, beautiful passion arises and then dies out, powerless, undirected, misunderstood or debased.' Early in the story the narrator observes that in St Petersburg, no one needs a face. I would think that this is true of London and most other great cities, and it is the kind of *aperçu*, typical of Chekhov, to which one returns over and over again in one's afterthoughts.

Chekhov once wrote that, 'I don't believe I have ever written a single line that has real literary value.' Perhaps this was defensive false modesty, or perhaps it was an entertaining irony. Perhaps he actually meant it (which I greatly doubt), but in any case the proposition is most certainly false. This story, too long to be a short story and too short to be a novella, is nonetheless a wonderful piece of literature. I know this because I have read it several times, and it is only excellent writing that improves with rereading.

– Louis de Bernières, 2002

It was in September 1891 that Chekhov wrote to the editor of the journal *The Northern Herald*, 'I have a little story almost ready for you: it's in draft, but needs to be polished up and a clean copy made. The remaining work will take a week or two, no more. It's called "My Patient's Story". But I'm gripped by doubts of a very serious nature: will it be passed by the censors?' The explanation for the title used in this early reference to *The Story of a Nobody* can be found in another of the author's letters dating from March 1893, the month when the story's second and concluding instalment appeared in the journal *Russian Thought*. 'I wanted to give it a little epilogue from myself,' wrote Chekhov to the writer and publisher Alexey Suvorin, 'with an explanation of how an unknown man's manuscript came into my possession, and I've written this epilogue, but I've put it aside until the book, i.e. until the time when the story comes out as a separate book.' However, Chekhov never published the story as a separate edition, and the early working title, meaningless without any frame written from the point of view of a doctor, was never used.

The provision of a suitable alternative title for the story proved no easy task for its author. Publication was already at hand when Chekhov wrote to the editor of *Russian Thought*, agreeing that 'My Patient's Story' would certainly not do ('it smells of the hospital' was his characteristically wry remark). He then listed seven further possible titles, of which some were rejected without comment ('Untitled' and 'A Tale with No Name'), others with brief justification ('In [St] Petersburg' – too dull, 'In the Eighties' – too pretentious, 'The Story of My Acquaintance' – too long). ' "The Manservant",' he wrote, 'doesn't correspond to the content and is crude.' The only title left was the one that, apparently *faute de mieux*, has continued to be used since its eleventh-hour adoption, and which has generally been rendered into English using the epithet 'anonymous' – 'An Anonymous Story', 'An Anonymous Man's Story' and the like. The English version 'The Story of a Nobody' not only avoids the stutter of these translations, but offers in addition an oblique reference to certain controversial elements of the story that worried Chekhov himself far more than the title.

The author's concerns about how the authorities would respond to his work were clear from the start. 'Although, it's true, my story doesn't preach harmful teachings,' he wrote in the letter of September 1891 cited above, 'still in the composition of its protagonists it may not please the censors. It's narrated by a former socialist, while figuring in it as character No. 1 is the son of the Deputy Minister of Internal Affairs. Both the socialist and the son of the Deputy Minister are quiet chaps and don't engage in politics in the story, but still I'm afraid, or at least consider it premature, to announce this story to the public.' A month later his doubts had turned to certainties, and publication of a story begun in 1887 was duly postponed for a further year and a half, with little abatement of his worries in the meantime.

Chekhov was, of course, by no means unique among Russian writers in his anticipation of problems with the censor. All the major figures of nineteenth-century Russian literature experienced such difficulties to some degree, and the years when Chekhov was working on this story were less than propitious for a narrative recounted by a self-confessed political activist. Following the abolition of serfdom in 1861, left-wing groups had increasingly made their presence felt in an empire where political opposition could prove fatal for both autocrats and revolutionaries, and their activities had culminated in 1881 with the assassination in the heart of the capital of the Tsar Liberator himself, Alexander II. His son and heir, Alexander III, took the inevitable reprisals, continuing the familiar Russian political cycle of alternating relaxation and repression, but, for all his government's efforts, Populism, Marxism and other brands of potential revolution flourished in the fertile Russian soil. In 1887 Alexander Ulyanov was executed for his part in a political assassination; and in 1893, just five months after the publication of *The Story of a Nobody*, his brother Vladimir, later to adopt the pseudonym Lenin, joined a Marxist intellectual group in St Petersburg and set off along the path to October 1917 and beyond. Little wonder, therefore, that Chekhov was cautious, even if his terrorist narrator was a figure inclined more towards inner turmoil than the propagation of dissent.

The title's definition of the narrator as a nobody immediately throws into relief his opposition to the prominent politician against whom he is plotting when the story opens, as the adjectives used to describe them are the positive and negative variants of one Russian word. An important aspect of the narrator's anonymity consists precisely in the fact that his life, in contrast to that of his target, has lacked significance. Now the hard lines of his devotion to the political cause which has hitherto supplied it with a framework are becoming increasingly blurred. His belief is undercut by a growing sense of the endlessly complex realities of the human condition, so often a theme in Chekhov. Thus, paradoxically, he comes increasingly to long for the security of that very life of a nobody. Being seriously ill, moreover, he is acutely aware of the proximity of death (another route to becoming a nobody), in the face of which all men, be they famous or unknown, masters or servants, are equal. The ageing statesman's farewell to the plotter on the one occasion they meet succinctly suggests the recognition of an unlikely fraternity between them.

Indeed, a story which appears set to investigate alternative and opposed world-views is remarkable for the way it operates rather in terms of parallels. If the narrator, the man-servant, has reservations about commitment, so too does the master, the self-centred womaniser Orlov; and certain features of each are also evident in the master's three friends: the pragmatist Pekarsky, the cowardly sycophant Kukushkin, and the ineffectual Gruzin. It is surely no coincidence that when the reader learns something of the narrator's true identity, it transpires that he bears the same patronymic, Ivanych, as his master: they are, in a metaphorical sense, brothers, both products of the same environment, both educated Russian gentlemen, and both ultimately at fault in the fate of the story's heroine, Zinaida Fyodorovna.

As elsewhere in the late nineteenth-century world, the position of women in society was a persistent question for debate in Russia, where female activists had by the 1890s already made their mark in radical politics. Chekhov's heroine, with her taste for domesticity and extravagance, is, like his narrator, by no means a revolutionary. But her readiness to engage in social struggle when thwarted in love gives a contemporary, perhaps ironic twist to the male-female relationships familiar from other works of Russian literature. Particularly significant in this respect are the novels of Ivan Turgenev, who is mentioned several times in the story. His repeated depiction of young women of great moral integrity, whose constancy and strength of will are contrasted with the weakness and inconsistency of the men who dominate their lives, finds echoes in a number of Chekhov's works. Yet in her volatility Zinaida might equally be seen as a descendant of the 'humiliated and insulted' inhabitants of St Petersburg depicted by Fyodor Dostoevsky, another writer referred to in the story, and perhaps also a literary source for a sick narrator with a propensity for dreams.

Shakespeare, the Russian national poet Alexander Pushkin and the verse playwright Alexander Griboedov are among a number of other writers quoted, misquoted and alluded to in Chekhov's story. The density of literary allusion is, however, less an example of artful narrative play – the entire story is, after all, narrated not by a novelist, but by a retired naval officer – than a realistic recognition of the significance of creative writers in moulding the patterns of thought of educated Russian society as a whole.

Fleeting references in Chekhov's letters might suggest that he was less than satisfied with the story. According to one letter it is at best 'tolerable', according to another it was difficult to write and would improve his finances without increasing his fame. He wrote in most detail to Alexey Suvorin, specifically about the story's ending: 'You won't like the conclusion, because I've messed it up. It should have been a bit longer. But there would have been a danger in writing it too long as well, for the characters are few, and when the same two people keep appearing for page after page it gets boring and those two people get blurred.' Elsewhere the author remarked that the ending lacked tension, with the action just flowing along smoothly and naturally. These comments in fact suggest that Chekhov was fully in control of his material and knew precisely what the conclusion demanded. He blamed the perceived deficiencies on the need for haste, but this was the voice of a perfectionist, and it is unlikely that the modern reader will concur with the self-criticism which he regularly applied to acknowledged masterpieces. One of the enduring attractions of Chekhov's plays lies in their simultaneous illumination of both the specific problems of the Russia that he knew, and the universal questions that confront all who encounter the works. The same can be said of many of his short stories too, and *The Story of a Nobody* can certainly be considered to fall into this category.

— *Hugh Aplin, 2002*

The Story of a Nobody

For reasons which it is not now the time to discuss in detail, it was necessary for me to become manservant to a certain official in St Petersburg by the name of Orlov. He was about thirty-five years old and was called Georgy Ivanych.[1]

I entered the service of this Orlov because of his father, the famous statesman, whom I considered a serious enemy of my cause. I calculated that by living in the son's house, from the conversations I would hear and from the papers and notes I would find on the desk, I could study in detail the plans and intentions of the father.

At about eleven o'clock in the morning the electric bell in the servants' hall would usually crackle to let me know that the master was awake. When I entered the bedroom with clean clothes and boots, Georgy Ivanych would be sitting motionless in bed, not so much still sleepy as wearied by his sleep, gazing into space and displaying no pleasure at having woken up. I helped him to dress, and he submitted to me grudgingly, silently, and without acknowledging my presence; then, with his head wet from washing and smelling of fresh scent, he went to the dining-room to have coffee. He sat at the table, drinking his coffee and leafing through the newspapers while the housemaid, Polya, and I stood by the door watching him. Two adults were obliged to watch with the gravest attention while a third drank coffee and gnawed at rusks. In all probability this was silly and very odd, but I saw nothing humiliating for myself in the fact that I had to stand by the door, although I was just as much an educated man and gentleman as Orlov himself.

My consumptive illness was then just beginning, and with it something else too that was perhaps rather more important than consumption. I do not know whether it was under the influence of the illness or of a change that was already under way, as yet unnoticed, in my outlook, but I was increasingly possessed from day to day by a passionate, nagging desire for the ordinary life of an ordinary person. I wanted peace of mind, health, good air, a full stomach. I was becoming a dreamer and, like a dreamer, did not know what it actually was that I needed. At times I wanted to retreat to a monastery, sit there for days on end by a window and gaze at the trees and fields; at other times I imagined myself buying a few acres of land and living like a country squire; at others I swore to myself that I would take up academic work and without fail become a professor at some provincial university. I am a retired lieutenant of the Russian navy, and I dreamed of the sea, our squadron and the corvette on which I had sailed all around the world. I wanted to experience once more that inexpressible feeling when, while walking through a tropical forest or watching the sunset in the Bay of Bengal, you are transfixed in rapture, yet at the same time yearn for your homeland. I dreamed of mountains, women, music, and with curiosity, like a boy, I looked closely at faces and listened intently to voices. And when I stood by the door watching Orlov drinking his coffee, I felt myself to be not a servant, but a man for whom everything in the world was of interest, even Orlov.

Orlov's looks were typical for St Petersburg: narrow shoulders, an elongated waist, sunken temples, eyes of indefinite colour, and sombrely tinted hair of meagre growth, on head, beard and moustache. His face was sleek, scrubbed and unpleasant. It was especially unpleasant when he was deep in thought or asleep. But there is no real need to describe commonplace looks; what is more, St Petersburg is not Spain, men's looks have no great significance here even in matters of

4

love and only imposing servants and coachmen need them. I mentioned Orlov's face and hair merely because there was something in his looks worthy of comment: that is, when Orlov picked up a newspaper or a book, no matter what it was, or when he met people, no matter who they were, there would appear in his eyes an ironic smile and his entire face would take on an expression of light, unmalicious mockery. Before reading or hearing anything he would always have irony already prepared like the shield of a savage. This was an habitual irony, long-held, and it had recently begun to appear on his face without any participation of his will, as if, it seemed, by reflex action. But more on this later.

After midday, with an ironic expression, he would pick up his briefcase stuffed with papers and leave for the office. He dined out and returned after eight. I lit the lamp and the candles in the study and he sat down in his armchair, stretched his feet out onto another chair and, sprawling in this fashion, began reading. Almost every day he brought new books home with him or they would be sent from the shops, and in the servants' hall, in the corners and under my bed, there lay a mass of books in three languages, not counting Russian, that had been read and discarded. He read with unusual speed. Tell me what you read, they say, and I will tell you who you are. That may be so, but to judge anything about Orlov from the books he read is absolutely impossible. It was just a mishmash. Philosophy and French novels, political economy and finance, new poets and cheap 'Intermediary' editions – and he read everything equally quickly and always with that same ironic expression in his eyes.

After ten he would dress carefully, often in a tailcoat, very rarely in the court uniform of a Gentleman of the Bedchamber, and leave the house. He would return towards morning.

5

We lived together quietly and peaceably and we had no misunderstandings. He did not usually notice my presence and when he did speak to me there was no ironic expression on his face – evidently he did not consider me a person.

Only once did I see him angry. One day – it was a week after I entered his service – he returned from some dinner at about nine o'clock looking tired and pettish. When I followed him into the study to light the candles he said to me, 'Something in the flat stinks.'

'No, the air is quite fresh,' I replied.

'And I'm telling you it stinks,' he repeated irritably.

'I open the windows every day.'

'Don't argue, you idiot!' he shouted. I was offended and was about to protest, and God knows how it would have ended if Polya, who knew her master better than I, had not intervened.

'It's true, what a horrible smell!' she said, raising her eyebrows. 'Where can it be coming from? Stepan, open the windows in the room and stoke up the fire.'

She began to huff and puff and set off around all the rooms, rustling her skirts and hissing with an airspray. But Orlov was still in a bad mood; he was clearly restraining himself from raging out loud, sitting at his desk and writing a letter at speed. After writing a few lines he snorted angrily and tore the letter up, then began writing again.

'Damn them!' he muttered. 'They expect me to have an unbelievable memory!'

Finally the letter was written; he rose from the desk and said, turning to me, 'You'll go to Znamenskaya Street and hand this letter to Zinaida Fyodorovna Krasnovskaya in person. But first of all ask the doorman whether her husband has returned, Mr Krasnovsky, that is. If he has returned, then hold on to the letter and come back. Wait!... If she should ask whether I have guests, then you will tell her that two gentlemen of some sort have been sitting with me since eight o'clock writing something.'

I went to Znamenskaya Street. The doorman told me that Mr Krasnovsky had not yet returned, and I set off for the second floor. The door was opened by a tall, fat, swarthy servant with black side-whiskers. In a sleepy, sluggish and rude way such as only a servant can use when speaking to another servant he asked me what I wanted. Before I had time to reply, a lady in a black dress walked rapidly into the hall from the drawing-room. She squinted at me.

'Is Zinaida Fyodorovna at home?' I asked.

'That's me,' said the lady.

'A letter from Georgy Ivanych.'

She opened the letter impatiently, and holding it in both hands, which allowed me to see her diamond rings, she started to read. I examined her white face with soft lines, a prominent chin and long, dark eyelashes. Looking at her, I would have guessed this lady to be no older than twenty-five.

'Convey my greetings and thanks,' she said when she had finished reading. 'Does Georgy Ivanych have guests?' she asked gently, joyfully and as if ashamed of her distrust.

'Two gentlemen of some sort,' I replied. 'They're writing something.'

'Convey my greetings and thanks,' she repeated and, with her head tilted to one side and reading the letter as she went, she left noiselessly.

I met few women at that time, and this lady, whom I saw but fleetingly, made an impression on me. While returning home on foot I recalled her face and the smell of her subtle perfume and I dreamed. When I got back, Orlov had already gone out.

2

And so I lived quietly and peaceably with my master, but nevertheless the dishonour and insult that I so feared when going into service were to be seen and made themselves felt every day. I did not get on with Polya. She was a well-fed, spoilt creature who adored Orlov because he was the master and despised me because I was the servant. From the point of view of a genuine servant or cook she was probably quite seductive: rosy cheeks, an upturned nose, narrowed eyes, and a fullness of figure which was already turning to plumpness. She used powder, painted her eyebrows and lips, laced herself into a corset and wore a bustle and a coin bracelet. She took short, bouncy steps; when she walked she rotated or, as they say, waggled her shoulders and backside. The rustling of her skirts, the cracking of her corset and the ringing of her bracelet, and that common smell of lipstick, toilet vinegar and scent, stolen from the master, aroused in me, when I cleaned the flat with her in the mornings, the feeling that I was doing something disgusting with her.

Either because I did not join her in thieving, or did not express any desire to become her lover, which probably insulted her, or perhaps because she sensed in me a different sort of person, she hated me from the very first day. My clumsiness, my appearance, not befitting a servant, and my illness seemed pitiful to her and roused in her a feeling of aversion. I was coughing a lot then and it was sometimes the case that I prevented her sleeping at night as her room and mine were separated by just a single wooden partition, and every morning she would say to me, 'I couldn't sleep again because of you. You should be in hospital, not living in gentlemen's houses.'

She believed so sincerely that I was not a person, but something immeasurably inferior to her, that, like matrons in Ancient Rome who felt no shame at bathing in the presence of slaves, she sometimes walked about in front of me wearing just a chemise.

One day at dinner (every day we received soup and roast meat from a porterhouse) when I was in an excellent, dreamy mood I asked, 'Polya, do you believe in God?'

'Well of course!'

'I suppose you believe in the Last Judgement,' I continued, 'and that we'll be answerable to God for each of our misdeeds?'

She did not reply and only made a scornful grimace. Looking on this occasion at her smug, cold eyes I realised that for this compact, fully-rounded nature there existed no God, no conscience, no laws, and that if I needed to murder, commit arson or steal, then money could not find me a better accomplice.

In a strange environment, and particularly as I was unused to overfamiliar modes of address and continual lying (saying 'the master is out' when he was at home), I found things difficult during my first week with Orlov. Wearing a servant's tailcoat I felt as if I were in armour. But then I got used to it. Like a genuine servant I served, tidied the flat, ran and rode around on various errands. When Orlov did not feel like going to a rendezvous with Zinaida Fyodorovna or when he forgot that he had promised to visit her, I would go to Znamenskaya Street, hand a letter to her there in person and lie. And as a result things turned out completely differently to the way I had expected when becoming a servant; each day of this new life of mine turned out to be wasted, both for me and for my cause, since Orlov never spoke about his father, and neither did his guests, and of the activities of the famous statesman. I knew only what I succeeded in gleaning, as previously, from newspapers and correspondence with comrades. The hundreds of notes and papers that I found and read in the study bore not even a distant relation to what I was seeking. Orlov was utterly indifferent to the grand deeds of his father and looked as if he had never heard of them, or as if his father were long dead.

3

On Thursdays we had guests.

I would order a piece of roast beef from a restaurant and speak on the telephone with the Yeliseyev delicatessen to get them to send us caviar, cheese, oysters, and so on. I would buy playing cards. In the morning Polya would start preparing the crockery for tea and the dinner service. To tell the truth, this little bit of activity added some variety to our idle life and Thursdays were the most interesting days for us.

Only three guests came. The most weighty and perhaps the most interesting was the one by the name of Pekarsky, a tall, lean man of about forty-five with a long hooked nose, a bushy black beard and a bald head. His eyes were large and bulging and he had the serious, pensive expression of a Greek philosopher. He served on the board of a railway and in a bank, he was a legal consultant in some important official organisation and engaged in business relations with a large number of private individuals as a guardian, competition chairman and so on. The rank he held was not at all a high one and he modestly called himself a barrister, yet he had enormous influence. His visiting card or note was sufficient to get you seen out of turn by an eminent doctor, the director of a railway or an important civil servant; it was said that with his patronage it was possible to get a government post even as high as the fourth grade and to hush up any unpleasant business at all. He was considered a very intelligent man, but his was a rather particular, strange intelligence. He could multiply 213 by 373 in his head in a flash or convert sterling to marks without the aid of a pencil and tables, he had an excellent knowledge of the railway business and finance, and he knew all there was to know about anything concerning administration; in civil cases, so they said, he was a most skilled lawyer and arguing a suit with him was a difficult business. But for this extraordinary intelligence many things that even a stupid man knows were quite incomprehensible. Thus he could not understand at all why it is that people get bored, cry, shoot themselves and even kill others, why they worry about things and events that do not affect them personally, and why they laugh when they read Gogol or Saltykov-Schedrin. Everything abstract and evanescent in the sphere of thought and feeling was incomprehensible to him and boring, like music for someone who has no ear. He looked at people only from a business point of view and divided them into the capable and the incapable. No other division existed for him. Honesty and decency are simply a sign of capability. Carousing, card-playing and debauchery are permissible, but only so long as they do not affect business. It is silly to believe in God, but religion should be protected as it is essential for the people to have some restraining principle, otherwise they will not work. Punishments are necessary only as a deterrent. There is no reason to make the trip out to a country house, as it is fine in town too. And so on. He was a widower and had no children, yet lived his life on an expansive family scale and

11

paid three thousand a year for his flat.

The second guest, Kukushkin, a youthful fourth-grade civil servant, was a short man distinguished by an extremely unpleasant expression, given him by the disproportion of his fat, flabby body and his small, lean face. His lips were heart-shaped and his little clipped moustache looked as if it had been stuck on with lacquer. He was a man with the mannerisms of a lizard. He did not walk into a room, but somehow crawled in, taking tiny little steps, rocking and tittering, and when he laughed he would bare his teeth. He was an officer for special commissions at the service of somebody or other and did nothing, although he had a large income, especially in summer when various official trips were invented for him. He was a careerist, not to the marrow but deeper, to his last drop of blood, and a petty careerist at that, unsure of himself and building his career just on handouts. For the sake of some minor foreign decoration, or so that it would be in the newspapers that he had attended a requiem mass or service of prayer with other high-ranking figures, he was prepared to undergo any humiliation at all, beg, flatter, make promises. Out of cowardice he flattered Orlov and Pekarsky, because he thought them powerful men; he flattered Polya and me because we were servants to an influential man. Every time I took his fur coat he would titter and ask me, 'Stepan, are you married?' – and then there would follow some indecent vulgarities – the mark of his special attention to me. Kukushkin flattered Orlov's weaknesses, his spoiled and smug nature; so that Orlov would like him he pretended to be a malicious scoffer and atheist and joined him in criticising people before whom he had been servile and sanctimonious elsewhere. When the talk at dinner was of women and love he pretended to be a subtle and sophisticated libertine. In general, it should be noted, St Petersburg playboys enjoy talking about their unusual tastes. Some youthful fourth-grade civil servant is perfectly satisfied with the caresses of his cook or some unfortunate girl who walks Nevsky Avenue, but to listen to him you would think him infected with all the vices of both East and West, an honorary member of a full dozen reprehensible secret societies and already in the bad books of the police. Kukushkin lied about himself brazenly, and it was not so much that people did not believe him, as that they paid no attention to any of his cock-and-bull stories.

The third guest, Gruzin, the son of a respected and learned general, was the same age as Orlov, a long-haired blond with bad eyesight who wore gold spectacles. I can remember his long, pale fingers, like those of a pianist; and in his figure as a whole there was something of the musician, of the virtuoso. In orchestras such figures play the first violin. He had a cough and suffered from migraines and generally seemed sickly and weak. At home he was probably undressed and dressed like a child. He had graduated from a college of jurisprudence and worked at first in a legal department, then he was transferred to the Senate, but he left; thanks to patronage he was given a post in the Ministry of State Property, but again soon left. During my time he was in charge of a desk in Orlov's section, but would talk about soon transferring back to the legal department. His attitude to work and to his moves from one post to another was exceptionally frivolous, and when people talked in his presence about ranks, awards, salaries, he would give a good-natured smile and repeat Prutkov's[2] aphorism, 'Only in the service of the state will you learn the truth!' He had a small wife with a wrinkled face who was very jealous, and five skinny little children; he was unfaithful to his wife, loved his children only when he could see them, and in general had an indifferent attitude to his family and made fun of it. He and his family lived in debt, borrowing wherever and from whoever they could at every convenient opportunity, not even overlooking his superiors and doormen. He was a flaccid character, lazy to the point of complete indifference to himself, drifting with the current who knows where and why. Wherever he was led he would go. If he was taken to some dive, he would go; if he was given wine, he would drink, if he was not given it he would not drink; if wives were criticised in front of him, he too would criticise his own, claiming that she had ruined his life, but when they were praised, he also praised his, saying sincerely, 'I love her very much, the poor thing.' He had no fur coat, and he always wore a travelling blanket which smelt of the nursery. It was strange, but when at dinner he fell into thought about something, rolled pieces of bread into balls and drank a lot of red wine, I was almost certain that there was something in him, something he too probably felt vaguely within himself, but which, with all life's vanity and vulgarities, he did not have the time to understand and value. He played the piano a little. Sometimes he would sit down at the piano, strike two or three chords and quietly begin to sing, 'What does the coming day hold for me?'[3] – but, as if frightened, he would get up at once and move well away from the piano.

The guests usually gathered by ten o'clock. They played cards in Orlov's study, and Polya and I served them tea. Only here could I appreciate fully all the sweetness of being a servant. Standing by the door over the course of four or five hours, seeing that there were no empty glasses, changing the ashtrays, running to the table to pick up a piece of chalk or card that had been dropped, but, most important, standing, waiting, being attentive and not daring to speak, to cough, to smile, that, I can assure you, is harder than the hardest labour of a peasant. At one time I used to stand on watch for four hours at a stretch on stormy winter nights, and I think the watch incomparably easier.

They played cards until about two o'clock, sometimes until three, and then, stretching, went to the dining-room for supper or, as Orlov put it, to have a bite to eat. Over dinner, conversations. It usually began with Orlov starting to talk with laughing eyes about some acquaintance, about a book he had recently read, about a new appointment or project; the flatterer Kukushkin joined in, hitting the same note, and there began, given the mood I was then in, the most repulsive music. The irony of Orlov and his friends knew no bounds and showed mercy to nothing and to nobody. They spoke of religion – irony; they spoke of philosophy, of the meaning and objectives of life – irony; if someone raised the question of the common people – irony. In St Petersburg there is a special breed of men who occupy themselves specifically by poking fun at every aspect of life; they cannot pass by even a starving man or a suicide without some crude comment. Orlov and his comrades, however, did not joke and did not poke fun, but spoke with irony. They said that there is no God and that with death the individual disappears completely; immortals exist only in the French Academy. There is no true good and there cannot be, for its existence is conditional upon human perfection, and this latter is a logical absurdity. Russia is as boring and wretched a country as Persia. The intelligentsia is hopeless; in Pekarsky's opinion it consists in the over-whelming majority of the incapable and good-for-nothing. And the common people had turned to drink, grown lazy, become thieves and were degenerate. We have no science, our literature is clumsy, trade depends on swindling: 'no deceit –

15

no sale'. And all in similar vein, and all funny.

Towards the end of dinner things became jollier because of the wine and they moved on to jolly conversations. They made fun of Gruzin's family life, Kukushkin's conquests, or of Pekarsky, in whose book of expenses there was supposed to be a page with the heading: *On charitable business,* and another: *On physiological needs.* They said that there were no faithful wives; no wife from whom, given a certain skill, you could not win a kiss or two without leaving the drawing-room, while her husband sat next door in the study. Adolescent girls were debauched and already knew everything. Orlov had a letter from a fourteen-year-old schoolgirl; returning from school she had 'picked up a nice officer on Nevsky Avenue', who allegedly took her back to his place and let her go only late in the evening, and she had been quick to write to her girlfriend about this to share her raptures. They said there never had been purity of morals and there was none today, obviously it was unnecessary; mankind had managed perfectly well without it up until now, while the harm from so-called debauchery was undoubtedly exaggerated. The perversion provided for in our code of punishments had not prevented Diogenes from being a philosopher and teacher; Caesar and Cicero had been libertines and at the same time great men. As an old man Cato had married a young girl, and none the less continued to be considered a strict observer of fasts and a guardian of morals.

At three or four o'clock the guests went their separate ways or drove off together, either out of town, or to visit a certain Varvara Osipovna on Ofitserskaya Street, while I went back to my room in the servants' hall and for a long time could not get to sleep because of an aching head and my cough.

4

About three weeks after I entered Orlov's service, on a Sunday morning, as I recall, somebody rang at the door. It was not yet eleven o'clock, and Orlov was still asleep. I went to open the door. You can imagine my astonishment: outside on the landing stood a lady in a veil.

'Is Georgy Ivanych up?' she asked.

And from her voice I recognised Zinaida Fyodorovna, to whom I had taken letters on Znamenskaya Street. I cannot remember whether I had the time or was able to answer her – I was embarrassed by her arrival. What is more, she had no need of my reply. In a moment she had slipped past me and, filling the hall with the aroma of her perfume which to this day I still remember well, she went off into the flat and her footsteps fell quiet. For at least half an hour after that nothing could be heard. But again somebody rang at the door. This time a young girl dressed up to the nines, evidently a maid from a wealthy household, and our doorman, both panting, carried in two suitcases and a basket.

'These are for Zinaida Fyodorovna,' said the girl.

And she left without saying another word. This was all mysterious and elicited a sly smirk from Polya who was reverential towards the master's mischief; it was as if she wanted to say, 'What about us then!' and she went around on tiptoe all the time. Finally footsteps were heard; Zinaida Fyodorovna came quickly into the hall and, catching sight of me in the doorway of the servants' hall, said, 'Stepan, let Georgy Ivanych have his clothes.'

When I went in to Orlov with his clothing and boots he was sitting on the bed with his feet lowered onto the bear-skin rug. His entire figure expressed embarrassment. He disregarded me and was not interested in any opinion I held as a servant: he was evidently embarrassed and confused before himself, before his 'inner eye'. He dressed, washed and then busied himself with his brushes and combs in silence and unhurriedly, as though giving himself time to think over his situation and make sense of it, and it was noticeable, even from looking at his back, that he was embarrassed and dissatisfied with himself.

They had coffee together. Zinaida Fyodorovna poured from the coffee-pot for herself and for Orlov, then put her elbows on the table and laughed.

'I still can't believe it,' she said. 'When you're on a long journey and then you arrive at a hotel, you still can't believe that you don't have to travel any more. It's nice to heave a little sigh.'

With the expression of a small girl who very much wants to be naughty she heaved a little sigh and once again laughed.

'You'll forgive me,' said Orlov, nodding at the newspapers. 'Reading over coffee is a habit of mine that can't be broken. But I can do two things at once, both read and listen.'

'Carry on reading. Your habits and your freedom will remain yours. But why such a glum physiognomy? Are you always like this in the mornings or is it just today? Aren't you glad?'

'On the contrary. But I admit I am a little shocked.'

'Why? You had time to prepare for my invasion. I threatened you every day.'

'Yes, but I didn't expect you to carry out your threat actually today.'

'And I didn't expect it myself, but it's better this way. It's better, my dear. Pull out an aching tooth straight away and there's an end to it.'

'Yes, of course.'

'Oh, my darling!' she said, screwing up her eyes. 'All's well that ends well, but before it ended well, how much trouble there was! Pay no attention to my laughing; I'm glad, I'm happy, but I feel more like crying than laughing. Yesterday I survived a real battle,' she continued in French. 'But God alone knows how hard it was for me. Yet I'm laughing because I can't believe it. It seems to me that I'm sitting drinking coffee with you not in real life, but in a dream.'

Then, continuing in French, she told how the day before she had left her husband, and her eyes were at one moment filled with tears, and at the next laughing as she looked with delight at Orlov. She told how her husband had long suspected her, but had avoided serious discussion; quarrels were extremely frequent, and usually at their very height he would abruptly fall silent and go off to his study in case in a fit of temper he should suddenly give voice to his suspicions and in case she herself should begin a serious talk. Zinaida Fyodorovna meanwhile felt guilty, worthless, incapable of a bold, significant step, and as a result with every day hated herself and her husband more, and was tormented as if in hell. But the day before, during a quarrel, when he shouted in a plaintive voice, 'My God, when will this all end?', and went off to his study, she chased after him like a cat after a mouse and, preventing him from closing the door behind him, she shouted that she hated him with all her being. Then he let her into the study and she told him everything, admitted that she loved another man, that this other man was her true, most lawful husband, and that she felt it the duty of her conscience to go to him this very day, no matter what, even if cannon-shot were to be fired at her.

'The romantic vein beats strongly in you,' Orlov interrupted her without raising his eyes from the newspaper.

She laughed and continued her story without touching her coffee. Her cheeks were burning, this embarrassed her a little and she threw confused glances at me and at Polya. From the rest of her story I learned that her husband answered her with reproaches, threats, and finally with tears, and it would be truer to say that it was not she, but he that survived a battle.

'Yes, my dear, so long as my nerves were on edge, everything went fine,' she recounted, 'but as soon as the night came on my spirits fell. You don't believe in God, Georges, but I do have a little faith and I'm afraid of retribution. God demands of us patience, magnanimity, self-sacrifice, and here am I refusing to be patient and wanting to arrange life in my own way. Is that a good thing? And what if from God's point of view it's a bad thing? At two o'clock in the morning my husband came into my room and said, "You won't dare to leave. I'll demand your return, the police will be involved, there'll be a scandal." And a little later I see him standing in the doorway again like a shadow. "Have pity on me. Your leaving might do me harm at work." These words had a nasty effect on me, as if they had eaten into me, I thought that this was the beginning of retribution, and I started to tremble in fear and cry. It seemed as if the ceiling would crash down on top of me, I would be taken away to the police station at any moment, you would stop loving me – in a word, God knows what! I'll go away, I thought, to a convent or to be a sick-nurse somewhere, I'll give up happiness, but then I remembered that you love me and that I have no right to make decisions about myself without your knowledge, and everything began to get confused in my head, and I was in despair, not knowing what to think or do. But the sun came up and I felt more cheerful again. I waited until morning and turned up here.

Oh, how I've suffered, my darling! Two nights running I've not slept!'

She was weary and excited. She wanted at one and the same time to sleep and to talk endlessly, to laugh and to cry and to go to a restaurant for breakfast so that she could feel herself free.

'Your flat is cosy, but I'm afraid it will be too small for two,' she said, quickly going around all the rooms after her coffee. 'Which room will you let me have? I like this one because it's next door to your study.'

After one o'clock she changed her clothes in the room next to the study which afterwards she started calling hers, and went out with Orlov for breakfast. They also had dinner in a restaurant, and in the long gap between breakfast and dinner they drove around the shops. Until late in the evening I kept opening the door to assistants and messengers from the shops and taking delivery from them of various purchases. Among other things they bought a splendid cheval-glass, a dressing-table, a bed and a luxury tea-service which we did not need. They bought an entire set of copper saucepans which we stood in a row on a shelf in our empty, cold kitchen. When we were unwrapping the tea-service, Polya's eyes lit up and she glanced at me two or three times with hatred, afraid that perhaps not she, but I would be the first to steal one of these graceful little cups. They bought a lady's writing-desk, very expensive but awkward. Obviously Zinaida Fyodorovna intended to settle down here firmly as the mistress.

She and Orlov returned some time after nine. Filled with the proud consciousness that she had done something bold and extraordinary, loving passionately and, as it seemed to her, passionately loved, languorous and looking forward to a deep and happy sleep, Zinaida Fyodorovna was revelling in her new life. In an excess of happiness she clasped her hands tightly together, affirmed that everything was fine, and swore that she would love eternally, and these vows and the naive, almost childish certainty that she too was deeply loved and would be loved eternally, made her look about five years younger. She talked charming nonsense and laughed at herself.

'There is no greater good than freedom!' she said, forcing herself to say something serious and meaningful. 'After all, how absurd, when you think about it! We attach no value to our own opinion, even if it is an intelligent one, but tremble before the opinion of various fools. Until the last minute I was afraid of the opinion of others, but as soon as I listened to myself and decided to live in my own way, my eyes were opened, I conquered my foolish fear and now I am happy and wish everyone similar happiness.'

But her train of thought was broken straight away and she talked of a new flat, of wallpaper, horses, of a journey to Switzerland and Italy. Orlov, meanwhile, was exhausted by the trip to the restaurants and shops and continued to feel the embarrassment before himself that I had noticed in him that morning. He smiled, but more from politeness than pleasure, and whenever she spoke seriously about anything he would agree ironically, 'Oh yes!'

'Stepan, find a good cook quickly,' she said, turning to me.

'There's no need to hurry with the kitchen,' said Orlov, glancing at me coldly. 'First of all we must move to a new flat.'

He never kept a kitchen or horses where he lived because, as he put it, he did not like to 'get things dirty at home', and he suffered Polya and me in his flat only out of necessity. The so-called hearth and home with its customary joys and irritations was an insult to his tastes, just like vulgarity; to be pregnant or to have children and talk about them – that was bad form, common. And I was now extremely curious to see how these two creatures would get on together in the same flat – she, home-loving and domesticated, with her copper saucepans and with dreams of a good cook and horses, and he, who often told his friends that in the flat of a respectable, decent man, as on a warship, there should be nothing superfluous – neither women, nor children, neither bits of clothing, nor kitchen utensils...

5

Next I shall tell you what happened the following Thursday. On that day Orlov and Zinaida Fyodorovna dined out in a restaurant, either Contant's or Donon's. Orlov returned home alone, while Zinaida Fyodorovna, as I learned later, went to visit her old governess on the other side of the Neva where she was to wait out the time while our guests were with us. Orlov did not want to show her to his friends. I realised this in the morning when he began over coffee to persuade her that for the sake of peace and quiet it was essential to call off his Thursdays.

The guests arrived as usual almost at the same time.

'And is the mistress at home?' Kukushkin asked me in a whisper.

'No sir,' I replied.

He went in with sly, unctuous eyes, smiling mysteriously and rubbing his hands from the cold.

'I have the honour of congratulating you,' he said to Orlov, his whole body trembling from his flattering, obsequious laughter. 'May you bear fruit and multiply as the cedars of

Lebanon.'

The guests set off for the bedroom and made jokes there about the women's shoes, the rug between the two beds and the grey blouse hanging on the bedhead. They found it amusing that a stubborn fellow who despised everything that was ordinary about love had suddenly been caught in a woman's nets in such a simple and ordinary way.

'What we didst mock, the same wouldst they serve,' was repeated several times by Kukushkin, who, incidentally, was unpleasantly pretentious in his parading of quotations from Church Slavonic. 'Quiet!' he whispered, raising a finger to his lips when they moved from the bedroom to the room next to the study. 'Sssh! Here Margareta dreams of her Faust.'

And he roared with laughter as if he had said something dreadfully funny. I looked intently at Gruzin, expecting his musical soul to be unable to bear this laughter, but I was mistaken. His kind, lean face was glowing with pleasure. Affecting a burr and choking with laughter, he remarked as they sat down to play cards that for the completion of his familial bliss it remained only for little Georgey to get himself a cherry-wood pipe and a guitar. Pekarsky had the occasional weighty laugh, but from his expression of concentration it was evident that he found Orlov's new love story unpleasant. He did not understand what exactly had happened.

'But what about the husband?' he asked, puzzled, when they had already played three rubbers.

'I don't know,' replied Orlov.

Pekarsky combed his bushy beard with his fingers, fell into thought and was silent from then on, right up until supper. When they had sat down to supper, he said slowly, drawing out every word:

'Excuse me, but in general I don't understand either of

you. You could have fallen in love with one another and broken the seventh commandment as much as you liked – that I can understand. Yes, I find that comprehensible. But why let the husband into your secrets? Is that really necessary?'

'Isn't that really all the same?'

'Hmm…' Pekarsky was thoughtful. 'This is what I'll say to you, my good friend,' he continued with an evident effort of thought. 'If I ever remarry and you take it into your head to cuckold me, then do it so that I don't notice. It's much more honest to deceive a man than to ruin the order in his life and his reputation. I understand. You both think that by living openly you are acting unusually honestly and liberally, but I cannot agree with this … what's it called? … with this romanticism.'

Orlov made no reply. He was in a bad mood and did not feel like talking. Pekarsky, still perplexed, tapped his fingers on the table, thought for a moment and said:

'All the same, I don't understand either of you. You're not a student and she isn't a seamstress. You're both people of means. I assume you could arrange a separate flat for her?'

'No, I couldn't. Read Turgenev.'

'Why should I read him? I've read him before.'

'Turgenev teaches in his works that every elevated, honest, thinking young woman should go away to the ends of the earth with the man she loves and serve his idea,' said Orlov, narrowing his eyes ironically. 'The ends of the earth – that is *licentia poetica*: the entire earth with all its ends fits into the flat of the man she loves. Therefore not living in the same flat with a woman who loves you means denying her her elevated purpose and not sharing her ideals. Yes, my dear, Turgenev wrote the recipe, now I have to eat it for him.'

'What Turgenev has to do with it I don't understand,' said

Gruzin quietly, shrugging his shoulders. 'But remember, Georgey, how in "Three Meetings" he's walking along late in the evening somewhere in Italy and suddenly he hears, *Vieni pensando a me segretamente!*[4] sang Gruzin. 'Marvellous!'

'But there was no force involved in her moving here, was there?' said Pekarsky. 'You wanted it yourself.'

'Well, there's an idea! Not only did I not want it, I could not even imagine this would ever happen. When she said she would move in with me I thought she was making a pleasant joke.'

Everyone laughed.

'I could not have wanted it,' continued Orlov, using a tone as if being forced to justify himself. 'I'm not one of Turgenev's heroes, and if at some time in the future I have to liberate Bulgaria[5], I won't need any female company. I regard love above all as a requirement of my organism, a base requirement alien to my spirit; it needs to be satisfied with reasoning, alternatively it should be completely denied, otherwise it will bring into your life just such impure elements as itself. To make it a pleasure and not a torment I try to make it beautiful and surround it with a great deal of illusion. I won't go to see a woman if I'm not certain in advance that she will be beautiful, fascinating; and I won't go to see her if I'm not on top form myself. And only under such conditions can we succeed in deceiving one another, and then we seem to be in love and we're happy. But can I want copper saucepans and uncombed hair or to be seen when I'm unwashed and in a bad mood? In the simplicity of her heart Zinaida Fyodorovna wants to make me love the thing I've been hiding from the whole of my life. She wants my flat to smell of cooking and kitchen-maids; she needs to make a lot of fuss moving to a new flat and drive around with her own horses; she needs to count my underwear and worry over my health; she needs to intervene in my private life at every moment and watch my every step, while at the same time sincerely assuring me that my habits and freedom will remain mine. She is convinced that, like newly-weds, we shall in the very near future go travelling, that is, she wants to be inseparable from me both in train compartments and hotels, whereas when I'm on a journey I like to read and cannot bear conversation.'

'Well, enlighten her,' said Pekarsky.

'How? Do you think she'll understand me? I'm sorry, but our thinking is so different! In her opinion, leaving Mummy and Daddy or your husband for the man you love is the height of civic courage, while I think it's just childish. Falling in love and taking up with a man means starting a new life, while I think it means nothing. Love and a man make up the essence of her life, and perhaps in this respect the philosophy of the unconscious is working in her; you just try and convince her that love is only a simple requirement, like food or clothing, that the world doesn't come to an end at all because there are bad husbands and wives, that you can be a libertine, a seducer and at the same time a man of genius and nobility, or, on the other hand, you can refuse the pleasures of love and at the same time be a foolish, vicious animal. A cultured man of today, even one of low standing, a French workman for example, spends ten sous a day on dinner, five on wine with his dinner, and between five and ten on a woman, but his mind and his nerves he gives in their entirety to his work. Whereas Zinaida Fyodorovna gives not sous, but all her soul to her love. Perhaps I'll try and set her straight, but in reply she'll let out a sincere cry of anguish that I've destroyed her, that she has nothing left in her life.'

'Don't say anything to her,' said Pekarsky, 'just rent a

separate flat for her. And that's that.'

'It's easily said…'

They were silent for a little while…

'But she is sweet,' said Kukushkin. 'She is charming. Women like that imagine they will love for ever, and succumb with pathos.'

'But you need to have a head on your shoulders,' said Orlov, 'you need to reason. All the instances we know from daily life entered in the annals of countless novels and dramas unanimously confirm that decent people's various adulteries and cohabitations, no matter what the love was like at the beginning, don't last for more than two or at the most three years. She must know this. And that's why all these saucepans and moving and hopes for eternal love and concord are nothing more than the desire to fool herself and me. She is both sweet and charming – who's arguing? But she's upset the apple-cart of my life; what until now I had considered a trifle, nonsense, she is forcing me to elevate to the level of a serious question; I'm serving an idol that I never considered a god. She is both sweet and charming, but now for some reason my heart feels heavy when I'm riding home from work, as though I'm expecting to come across some inconvenience at home, such as stove-repairers who have dismantled all the stoves and piled up mountains of bricks. In a word, I'm no longer giving sous for love, but a part of my peace of mind and my nerves. And that's awful!'

'And she cannot hear this villain!' sighed Kukushkin. 'My dear sir,' he said theatrically, 'I shall release you from the burdensome duty of loving this charming creature! I shall win Zinaida Fyodorovna from you!'

'You may…' said Orlov casually.

For the best part of a minute Kukushkin's whole body

shook as he laughed a high-pitched laugh, and then he said, 'Watch out, I'm not joking! Don't start playing Othello later on!'

They all began talking of Kukushkin's tirelessness in matters of love, of how he was irresistible to women and dangerous to husbands and of how in the afterlife devils would roast him over coals for his dissolute life. He narrowed his eyes and was silent and when the names of female acquaintances were mentioned he wagged his little finger, as if to say 'don't give away other people's secrets'. Suddenly Orlov looked at the clock.

The guests understood and started to take their leave. I remember that Gruzin, fuddled after the wine, took an agonisingly long time on this occasion to get into his outdoor clothes. He put on his coat, reminiscent of those dressing-gowns that are made for children in poor families, pulled up the collar and began telling some long story; then, seeing that nobody was listening to him, he threw over his shoulder the travelling blanket that smelt of the nursery and with a guilty and beseeching look asked me to look for his hat.

'Georgey, my angel!' he said affectionately. 'Do as I say, my dear, let's go out of town now!'

'You can go, but I can't. I'm as good as married now.'

'She's wonderful, she won't be angry. My good kind boss, let's go! The weather's marvellous, the snow falling, the frost... Honestly, you need to give yourself a shake, or else you're in a bad mood, the devil knows...'

Orlov stretched, yawned and looked at Pekarsky.

'Will you come?' he asked in indecision.

'Don't know. Probably.'

'Perhaps I should get drunk, eh? Well, alright, I'll come,' Orlov decided after some hesitation. 'Wait, I'll go and get some money.'

He went into the study and Gruzin slouched after him with his travelling blanket trailing behind. A minute later both came back into the hall. A tipsy and very contented Gruzin was crumpling a ten-rouble note in his hand.

'We'll settle up tomorrow,' he said. 'And she's kind, she won't be angry... She's my little Liza's godmother, I love her, the poor thing. Oh, you dear man!' He suddenly burst into joyful laughter and his forehead fell onto Pekarsky's back. 'Oh Pekarsky my dear! King of the courts and a dry old stick, but I bet he likes women...'

'Add "fat ones",' said Orlov, putting on his fur coat. 'Anyway, let's go, or else, if we're not careful, we'll meet her on the way out.'

'*Vieni pensando a me segretamente!*' sang Gruzin.

Finally they left. Orlov did not sleep at home and returned the following day in time for dinner.

6

Zinaida Fyodorovna lost the little gold watch that had been given her once by her father. This loss surprised and frightened her. She spent half the day walking around all the rooms, examining the tables and window sills with an air of perplexity, but the watch had vanished into thin air.

Soon afterwards, about three days later, Zinaida Fyodorovna, returning home, left her purse by mistake in the hall. Luckily for me, it was not I that helped her take her things off on this occasion, but Polya. When the purse came to mind, it was no longer to be found in the hall.

'Strange!' said Zinaida Fyodorovna at a loss. 'I remember

very well, I took it out of my pocket to pay the cabman … and then put it down here by the mirror. It's the oddest thing!'

I had not taken it, but a feeling seized me as if I had stolen it and been caught. Tears even came into my eyes. As they were sitting down to dinner, Zinaida Fyodorovna said to Orlov in French, 'We've got ghosts in the flat. Today I lost my purse in the hall, but now, lo and behold, it's lying on my desk. But the ghosts didn't perform this trick for free. They took a gold coin and twenty roubles for their work.'

'First you lose your watch, then your money…' said Orlov. 'Why does nothing like that ever happen to me?'

A minute later Zinaida Fyodorovna had already forgotten about the trick that the ghosts had performed and was laughing as she told how last week she had ordered herself some writing-paper, but had forgotten to provide her new address, and the shop had sent the paper to the old flat, where her husband had been obliged to pay the bill of twelve roubles. And suddenly she let her gaze fall on Polya and looked at her intently. At the same time she blushed and became embarrassed to such an extent that she began talking about something else.

When I took coffee into the study, Orlov was standing by the fireplace with his back to the fire and she was sitting in the armchair opposite him.

'I'm not in a bad mood at all,' she said in French. 'But now I've begun to understand, and everything is clear to me. I can tell you the day and even the hour when she stole my watch. And the purse? Here there can be no doubt. Oh!' she laughed as she took her coffee from me. 'Now I understand why I lose my handkerchiefs and gloves so often. As you wish, but tomorrow I'm going to let this magpie go free and I'll send Stepan to fetch my Sofya. She's not a thief, and she doesn't

31

look so... repellent.'

'You're out of sorts. You'll be in a different mood tomorrow and you'll realise that you can't get rid of somebody just because you suspect them of something.'

'I don't suspect, I'm certain,' said Zinaida Fyodorovna. 'When I suspected this proletarian with the miserable face, your manservant, I didn't say a word. It's hurtful, Georges, that you don't believe me.'

'If you and I think differently about some subject, then that doesn't mean that I don't believe you. Maybe you're right,' said Orlov, turning to the fire and throwing in his cigarette, 'but all the same you shouldn't get agitated. In general, I admit, I didn't expect my little household to cause you so many serious cares and worries. A gold coin has disappeared, well never mind, have a hundred, if you like, from me, but changing the order of things, bringing in a new maid off the street, waiting for her to settle down – all that is a long, boring process and not in my character. The present maid is fat, it's true, and possibly has a weakness for handkerchiefs and gloves, but on the other hand she is perfectly respectable, disciplined, and doesn't squeal when Kukushkin pinches her.'

'In short, you cannot part with her... Just say so.'

'Are you jealous?'

'Yes, I'm jealous!' said Zinaida Fyodorovna decisively.

'Thank you.'

'Yes, I'm jealous!' she repeated, and tears began to shine in her eyes. 'No, it's not jealousy, but something worse... it's hard to give it a name.' She put her hands to her temples and continued with passion, 'You men can be so vile! It's awful!'

'I don't see anything awful here.'

'I've not seen it, I don't know, but they say that you men begin with maids even as children and later on you're already used to it and don't feel any disgust. I don't know, I don't know, but I've even read...Georges, you're right of course,' she said, going up to Orlov and changing her tone to one that was affectionate and pleading, 'I really am out of sorts today. But you must understand, I can't help it. I find her offensive and I'm afraid of her. It's hard for me just seeing her.'

'Surely you can rise above such trivia?' said Orlov, shrugging his shoulders in perplexity and moving away from the fireplace. 'After all, there's nothing simpler: take no notice of her and she won't be offensive, and you won't have to make a whole drama out of nothing.'

I left the study and do not know what reply Orlov received. In any event Polya remained with us. After this Zinaida Fyodorovna no longer turned to her for anything and evidently tried to manage without her services; whenever Polya handed her something or even just passed by with her bracelet jangling and her skirts crackling, she would wince.

I think if Gruzin or Pekarsky had asked Orlov to dismiss Polya, then he would have done so without the slightest hesitation and without troubling himself with any explanations; he was compliant, like all indifferent people. But for some reason in his relations with Zinaida Fyodorovna, even in trifling matters, he demonstrated an obstinacy which at times went as far as petty tyranny. And so I knew for sure: if Zinaida Fyodorovna liked something, then he definitely would not like it. When she came back from the shop and rushed to show off her new purchases to him, he would glance at them briefly and say coldly that the more superfluous things there were in the flat, the less air there would be. There were times when he had already put on his tailcoat to go somewhere and said goodbye to Zinaida Fyodorovna, but then suddenly out of obstinacy stayed at home. It seemed to me then that he stayed at home only to feel unhappy.

'Why have you stayed?' said Zinaida Fyodorovna, feigning disappointment, but at the same time glowing with pleasure. 'Why? You're not used to staying at home in the evenings, and I don't want you to betray your habits for my sake. Please go, unless you want me to feel I'm to blame.'

'Is anyone actually blaming you, then?' said Orlov.

With the look of a victim he sprawled in his armchair in the study and, shading his eyes with his hand, took up a book. But the book soon fell from his hands, he turned heavily in the armchair and again shaded his eyes as if from the sun. Now he was the one to be disappointed that he had not gone.

'May I come in?' said Zinaida Fyodorovna, entering the study hesitantly. 'Are you reading? I was bored, so I came just for one moment... to have a look.'

I remember on one of these evenings she went in just like that, hesitantly and without reason, and sank onto the carpet at Orlov's feet, and it was clear from her timid, gentle movements that she did not understand his mood and was afraid.

'You're always reading...' she began cautiously, evidently wanting to flatter him. 'Do you know, Georges, the reason for your success? You're highly educated and intelligent. What book is it?'

Orlov replied. Several minutes, which seemed to me very long, passed in silence. I stood in the drawing-room, from where I could observe them both, afraid to cough.

'I wanted to tell you something...' said Zinaida Fyodorovna softly and then laughed. 'Shall I? I expect you'll start to laugh and you'll call it self-deception. You see, I really, really want to think that you stayed at home today for my sake... to spend this evening together. Yes? Can I think that?'

'Think it,' said Orlov, shielding his eyes. 'The truly happy

34

person is the one who thinks not only about what is, but even about what is not.'

'What you just said was rather long and I didn't quite understand. That is, you mean happy people live through their imagination? Yes, that's true. I love sitting in your study in the evenings and letting my thoughts go far, far away… It's nice to dream sometimes. Let's dream out loud, Georges!'

'I didn't attend a girls' school and haven't studied that subject.'

'Are you in a bad mood?' asked Zinaida Fyodorovna, taking Orlov by the hand. 'Tell me why? When you're like this, I'm afraid. I can't tell whether you've got a headache or you're angry with me…'

Several more long minutes passed in silence.

'Why have you changed?' she said softly. 'Why are you never as tender and jolly now as you were on Znamenskaya Street? I've lived with you for almost a month, but it seems as if we've not yet started living and haven't yet talked about anything properly. Every time you answer me it's with little jokes or coldly and at great length like a teacher. And even in your little jokes there's something cold… Why have you stopped talking to me seriously?'

'I always talk seriously.'

'Well let's talk, then. For God's sake, Georges… Let's?'

'Alright. About what?'

'Let's talk about our life, about the future…' said Zinaida Fyodorovna dreamily. 'I'm always making plans for life, always making them – and I feel so good! Georges, I'll start with a question: when will you leave your job?'

'Why should I do that?' asked Orlov, removing his hand from his forehead.

'With views like yours you shouldn't be in the civil service.

You're out of place there.'

'My views?' asked Orlov. 'My views? By convictions and by nature I'm an ordinary civil servant, a character from Saltykov-Schedrin. You're mistaking me for someone else, I assure you.'

'Little jokes again, Georges!'

'Not at all. Perhaps my work doesn't satisfy me, but all the same it's better for me than anything else. I'm used to it there, the people there are just like me; at least I'm not superfluous there and I don't feel too bad.'

'You hate your work, it makes you feel sick.'

'Really? And if I resign and start dreaming out loud and fly off to another world, do you think that world will be less hateful to me than my job?'

'To contradict me you're even prepared to slander yourself,' said Zinaida Fyodorovna, offended, and stood up. 'I'm sorry I started this conversation.'

'Why are you angry? After all, I'm not angry because you don't work. Everyone lives as he wishes.'

'Do you really live as you wish? Are you really free? Writing papers all your life that run contrary to your convictions,' continued Zinaida Fyodorovna, clasping her hands in despair, 'doing as you're told, wishing your superiors a happy New Year, then cards, cards and more cards, and most important, serving an order that you cannot find attractive – no, Georges, no! Don't make such crude jokes. It's awful. You're a man of ideas and should serve only an idea.'

'Truly, you're mistaking me for someone else,' sighed Orlov.

'Just say you don't want to talk to me. You find me offensive, and that's that,' said Zinaida Fyodorovna through her tears.

'I'll tell you what, my dear,' said Orlov in an instructive tone, sitting up in his armchair. 'You were yourself so good as to remark that I am an intelligent and educated man, and teaching only spoils the scholar. All the ideas, great and small, that you have in mind when you call me a man of ideas, are well known to me. Therefore, if I prefer work and cards to these ideas, then I probably have grounds for doing so. That's the first thing. Secondly, as far as I'm aware, you've never worked, and your judgements on state service can only be derived from jokes and bad novellas. So it would do us no harm to agree once and for all not to talk about things that we've known for a long time or about things that don't enter the field of our competence.'

'Why are you talking to me like this?' said Zinaida Fyodorovna, retreating as if in horror. 'Why? Georges, come to your senses, for God's sake!'

Her voice froze and broke off; she was evidently trying to hold back her tears, but suddenly she burst into sobs.

'Georges, my darling, I'm lost!' she said in French, dropping down quickly in front of Orlov and resting her head on his knees. 'I'm exhausted, worn out and I can't go on, I can't... A depraved, hateful stepmother in my childhood, then my husband, and now you... you... You respond to my mad love with irony and coldness... And that dreadful, brazen maid!' she continued to sob. 'Yes, yes, I can see: I'm not a wife to you, not a friend, but a woman for whom you have no respect because she has become your lover... I shall kill myself!'

I did not expect these words and this crying to make such a powerful impression on Orlov. He blushed, moved restlessly in his armchair and in place of irony there appeared on his face the stupid terror of a little boy.

'My darling, you misunderstood me, I swear to you,' he mumbled in confusion, touching her hair and shoulders. 'Forgive me, I beg you. I was wrong and ... I hate myself.'

'I insult you with my complaints and whining ... You're an honest, generous... special person, and I'm conscious of that at every moment, but each day I've suffered anguish ...'

Zinaida Fyodorovna embraced Orlov impetuously and kissed him on the cheek.

'Only please don't cry,' he said.

'No, no ... I've already cried enough and I feel fine.'

'As far as the maid is concerned, tomorrow she'll no longer be here,' he said, still moving restlessly in his armchair.

'No, she must stay. Georges! Do you hear? I'm not afraid of her any more... I must rise above trivial matters and not have silly ideas. You're right! You're a special ... an extraordinary person!'

She soon stopped crying. Sitting on Orlov's lap, with teardrops still damp on her eyelashes, she recounted to him in a low voice something touching, something like memories of her childhood and youth, and stroked his face, while kissing his hands and examining them closely with their rings and charm bracelet. She was carried away by both her story and the nearness of the man she loved, and probably because of the fact that her recent tears had cleansed and refreshed her soul, her voice sounded unusually pure and sincere. And Orlov played with her chestnut hair and kissed her hands, soundlessly pressing his lips against them.

Later they drank tea in the study and Zinaida Fyodorovna read some letters out loud. They went to bed after midnight.

That night my side ached a lot, and right through until morning I could not get warm and fall asleep. I heard Orlov go past from the bedroom to his study. He sat there for about an hour, then rang. In my pain and tiredness I forgot about all social rules and proprieties and set off to the study barefooted, in just my underwear. Orlov was standing in the doorway waiting for me in his dressing-gown and nightcap.

'When you are called, you should appear dressed,' he said sternly. 'Bring some more candles.'

I meant to apologise, but suddenly began coughing violently and, so as not to fall, took hold of the doorpost with one hand.

'Are you ill?' asked Orlov.

I think this was the first occasion in all the time we had known one another that he had addressed me in a polite tone. God knows why. In my underwear and with my face contorted by coughing I probably played my part badly and did not look much like a servant.

'If you're ill, why is it you work?'

'So as not to die of hunger,' I replied.

'How essentially foul it all is!' he said softly, walking towards his desk.

While I, having thrown on my frock-coat, set up and lit new candles, he sat by the desk with his legs stretched out on the armchair, cutting the pages of a book.

I left him engrossed in his reading, and the book no longer fell from his hands as it had in the evening.

7

Now, as I write these lines, my hand is restrained by the fear fostered in me since childhood of appearing sentimental and foolish; whenever I want to be affectionate and use endearments, I do not know how to be sincere. It is because of precisely that fear and my lack of practice that I am quite unable to express with complete clarity what was then taking place in my soul.

I was not in love with Zinaida Fyodorovna, but in the normal human feeling that I had for her there was much more vitality, freshness and joy than there was in Orlov's love.

Working in the mornings with shoe-brush or broom, I would await with my heart in my mouth the moment when I should at last hear her voice and footsteps. To stand and look at her while she drank coffee and then had breakfast, to hold her fur coat for her in the hall and put overshoes on her little feet while she held on to my shoulder, and then to wait until the doorman rang me from downstairs, to meet her at the door, rosy, cold and powdered with snow, to listen to her abrupt exclamations about the frost or the cabman – if only you knew how important all this was for me! I wanted to fall in love, to have my own family, I wanted my future wife to have just such a face, just such a voice. I dreamed over my dinner, in the street when I was sent anywhere, and at night when I could not sleep. Orlov fastidiously tossed aside women's bits of clothing, children, a kitchen, copper sauce-pans, but I gathered them all up and cherished them in my dreams, loved them, begged them of fate, and had visions of a wife, a nursery, garden paths, a little house ...

I knew that if I came to love her, I could not dare to expect such a miracle as reciprocal feelings, but this consideration did not worry me. In my modest, quiet emotion, resembling an ordinary attachment, there was neither jealousy of Orlov, nor even envy, since I understood that personal happiness for a cripple like me was possible only in dreams.

Whenever Zinaida Fyodorovna, waiting for her Georges, gazed motionless into a book in the night-time without turning a page, or when she winced and went pale because Polya was going through the room, I suffered along with her, and it occurred to me to cut open this nasty abscess soon, arrange for her to find out soon everything that was said here at supper on Thursdays – but how was it to be done? More and more often I was obliged to witness tears. In the first weeks she laughed and sang her little song, even when Orlov was out, but by the second month there was a dreary silence in the flat, broken only on Thursdays.

She flattered Orlov, and to win from him an insincere smile or a kiss, she would kneel before him and fawn upon him like a little dog. Passing a mirror, even when she was in very low spirits, she could not resist glancing at herself and adjusting her hair. It seemed strange to me that she still continued to take an interest in her costumes and go into raptures over her shopping. Somehow this did not accord with her sincere sadness. She kept up with fashion and had expensive dresses made. For whom and for what purpose? Especially memorable for me was one new dress that cost four hundred roubles. To give four hundred roubles for a pointless, unnecessary dress, when Russian women hired by the day are paid twenty kopecks apiece for their drudgery with no food provided, and when lace-makers in Venice and Brussels get only half a franc a day each on the assumption that they will earn the remainder by depravity! And it was strange to me that Zinaida Fyodorovna was not conscious of this; it was disappointing. But she had only to leave the flat for me to forgive her everything, find an explanation for everything and wait for the doorman to ring me from downstairs.

She treated me as a servant, an inferior being. One can stroke a dog and at the same time not notice it; I was given orders, asked questions, but my presence was not noticed.

The master and mistress considered it improper to speak to me more than is normal; if, while serving at dinner, I had intervened in the conversation or started laughing, I would probably have been thought insane and would have been dismissed. But all the same Zinaida Fyodorovna was favourably disposed towards me. Whenever she sent me anywhere or explained how to deal with a new lamp or something of the sort, her face was unusually clear, kind and affable, and her eyes looked me right in the face. Each time this happened I thought that she remembered with gratitude how I used to bring her letters to Znamenskaya Street. Whenever she rang, Polya, who considered me her favourite and hated me for it, would say with a sarcastic smirk, 'Go on, *your lady* is calling you.'

Zinaida Fyodorovna treated me as an inferior being and did not suspect that if anybody in the household was degraded, then it was she and she alone. She did not know that I, a servant, suffered on her behalf and wondered twenty times or more daily what lay ahead for her and how this would all end. Things became noticeably worse with every day. After the evening when they talked about work, Orlov, who did not like tears, evidently began to fear and avoid conversations; whenever Zinaida Fyodorovna started to argue or beg or was on the point of crying, he would find a plausible excuse to go to his study or to leave the flat entirely. He spent the night at home more and more rarely and even more rarely did he dine in; on Thursdays it was he himself who now asked his friends to take him out somewhere. Zinaida Fyodorovna dreamed as before of her kitchen, a new flat and travelling abroad, but the dreams remained dreams. Dinner was brought from a restaurant, Orlov asked her not to raise the question of the flat until their return from abroad, and of the journey he said that it was impossible to go before he had grown his hair long, as hanging around hotels and working for an idea were impossible without long hair.

On top of it all, in Orlov's absence we started to have visits in the evenings from Kukushkin. There was nothing special in his behaviour, but I could never manage to forget the conversation when he stated his intention to win Zinaida Fyodorovna from Orlov. He was served tea and red wine while he tittered and, wanting to say something pleasant, gave the assurance that a free union was in every respect superior to one solemnised in church, and that in fact all decent people ought now to come to Zinaida Fyodorovna and bow down at her feet.

8

The Christmas holidays passed tediously in vague anticipation of something unpleasant. On New Year's Eve over the morning coffee Orlov announced unexpectedly that his superiors were dispatching him on a special mission to assist a senator who was carrying out an inspection of a certain province.

'I don't want to go, but I can't think up any excuse!' he said in vexation. 'I've got to go, there's nothing for it.'

At this news Zinaida Fyodorovna's eyes turned red in a moment.

'Will it be for long?' she asked.

'Five days or so.'

'I confess I'm glad you're going,' she said after some thought. 'You'll have some fun. You'll fall in love with someone during the trip and afterwards you can tell me about it.'

At every convenient opportunity she tried to let Orlov know that she was not restricting him in any way and that he could do whatever he liked, and this naive and utterly transparent policy fooled nobody, serving merely as another reminder to Orlov that he was not free.

'I'm leaving this evening,' he said and started to read the newspapers.

Zinaida Fyodorovna meant to accompany him to the station, but he dissuaded her, saying that he was not going to America, nor for five years, but only for five days or even less.

The farewells took place towards eight o'clock. He put one arm around her and kissed her on the forehead and on the lips.

'Be a good girl, don't get bored without me,' he said in an affectionate, heartfelt tone which touched even me. 'May the Lord preserve you.'

She gazed avidly into his face to impress his dear features the firmer in her memory, then gracefully put her arms around his neck and lay her head on his chest.

'Forgive me for our misunderstandings,' she said in French. 'A husband and wife cannot help but quarrel if they love one another, and I love you to the point of madness. Don't forget... Send frequent and detailed telegrams.'

Orlov kissed her again and went out, embarrassed, without a word. When the lock had clicked inside the door he stopped in thought halfway down the staircase and glanced up. It seemed to me that if so much as a single sound had carried to him from up the stairs at that moment, he would have gone back. But it was quiet. He adjusted his greatcoat and began hesitantly to go downstairs.

Cabs had already long been waiting by the entrance. Orlov got into one, and I with two suitcases into another. There was a hard frost and bonfires were smoking at the crossroads. Our speed meant the wind nipped at my face and hands and took my breath away; closing my eyes I thought what a marvellous woman she was! How she loved him! Nowadays even unwanted items are collected from courtyards and sold for charity, and broken glass is considered a good commodity, but a thing so valuable, so rare as the love of an elegant, young, bright and decent woman is utterly wasted. One old sociologist looked upon every negative passion as a power that, if you knew how, could be directed towards good, yet in Russia even a noble, beautiful passion arises and then dies out, powerless, undirected, misunderstood or debased. Why is it so?

The cabs halted unexpectedly. I opened my eyes and saw that we had stopped on Sergiyevskaya Street by the big house where Pekarsky lived. Orlov got out and disappeared into the entrance. After about five minutes Pekarsky's manservant appeared in the doorway without a hat and, angry because of the cold, shouted to me, 'Are you deaf or something? Let the cabs go and get upstairs. You're wanted!'

Not understanding a thing I set off up to the first floor. I had been in Pekarsky's flat before, that is I had stood in the hall and looked into the drawing-room, and after the damp, gloomy street I was always struck by the brilliance of its picture-frames, bronze and expensive furniture. Now in this brilliance I saw Gruzin, Kukushkin and, after a few moments, Orlov.

'Right, Stepan,' he said, coming towards me, 'I shall be staying here until Friday or Saturday. If there are any letters or telegrams, bring them here every day. At home you will say that I left, of course, sending regards. Off you go now.'

When I arrived home Zinaida Fyodorovna was lying on the

sofa in the drawing-room, eating a pear. There was just one candle burning in a candelabrum.

'You weren't late for the train?' asked Zinaida Fyodorovna.

'No, ma'am. The master sends his regards.'

I went to my room in the servants' hall and lay down as well. There was nothing to do, and I did not feel like reading. I was not surprised or indignant, but had to think hard to work out why this deception was found necessary. After all, only adolescent boys deceive their lovers this way. Could he, a man who had done a lot of reading and thinking, really not invent something a little cleverer? I admit I had quite a high opinion of his mind. I thought that if he found it necessary to deceive his minister or some other powerful person, he would use a great deal of energy and art to do so, but here, to deceive a woman, he was obviously happy with the first thing that came into his head; if the deception worked – good, if not – no harm done, and there would be no need to rack his brains to tell a second lie just as easily and quickly.

At midnight, when on the floor above us they greeted the New Year with the movement of chairs and shouts of 'hurrah', Zinaida Fyodorovna rang for me from the room next to the study. Listless from lying down for a long time, she was sitting at her desk, writing something on a scrap of paper.

'A telegram needs to be sent,' she said and smiled. 'Drive to the station quickly and ask them to forward it.'

Going outside a little later, I read the scrap of paper: 'Happy New Year! With it New Happiness! Telegraph soon, missing you terribly. Eternity already passed. Sorry cannot telegraph thousand kisses and heart. Enjoy yourself, darling. Zina.'

I sent the telegram and next morning handed her the receipt.

9

Worst of all was that Orlov thoughtlessly let Polya too into the secret of his deception by ordering her to bring his shirts to Sergiyevskaya Street. After this she looked at Zinaida Fyodorovna gloatingly, with a hatred I found incomprehensible, and never stopped snorting with pleasure either in her room or in the hall.

'She's outstayed her welcome, her time's up!' she said in delight. 'She must realise it herself…'

She already sensed that Zinaida Fyodorovna would not be with us for much longer and, so as not to waste time, she pinched everything she set eyes on – scent-bottles, tortoise-shell hairpins, handkerchiefs, shoes. The day after New Year Zinaida Fyodorovna called me into her room and informed me in a low voice that her black dress was missing. And then she went around all the rooms, pale, with an alarmed and indignant look on her face, talking to herself, 'How? No, how? I mean, such insolence is unheard-of!'

At dinner she wanted to pour herself some soup, but could not – her hands were trembling. Her lips were trembling too. She kept glancing helplessly at the soup and the pasties, waiting for the trembling to stop, then suddenly could not contain herself and looked at Polya.

'You, Polya, may leave the room,' she said. 'Just Stepan is enough.'

'It's alright, ma'am, I'll stay, ma'am,' replied Polya.

'There's no need for you to stay here. Go away altogether… altogether!' continued Zinaida Fyodorovna, standing up in great agitation. 'You can find yourself another place. Leave at once!'

'I can't leave without the master's order. He hired me. As

he orders, so be it.'

'I give you orders too! I am the mistress here!' said Zinaida Fyodorovna, turning quite red.

'Maybe you are the mistress, but only the master can dismiss me. He was the one that hired me.'

'Don't dare to stay here another minute!' shouted Zinaida Fyodorovna and struck her knife against a plate. 'You're a thief! Do you hear?'

Zinaida Fyodorovna threw her napkin onto the table and quickly left the dining-room with a pitiful look of suffering on her face. Polya, sobbing loudly and complaining to herself, left as well. The soup and the hazel-grouse had gone cold. And now for some reason all this luxury food on the table from the restaurant seemed to me beggarly and criminal, like Polya. The most pitiful and criminal to look at were two pasties on a little plate. 'Today we'll be taken back to the restaurant,' they seemed to say, 'but tomorrow we'll be served up again for dinner to some civil servant or famous singer.'

'The high and mighty mistress, what do you know!' reached my ears from Polya's room. 'If I'd wanted, I'd have been a mistress like her ages ago, but I've got some shame! We'll see which of us leaves first! Yes!'

Zinaida Fyodorovna rang. She was sitting in her room, in a corner, with an expression as though she had been put in the corner as a punishment.

'Has a telegram come?' she asked.

'No, ma'am.'

'Ask the doorman, perhaps there's a telegram. Oh, and don't leave the house,' she said as I was going, 'I'm afraid of being left alone.'

After this I was obliged to run downstairs to the doorman almost hourly to ask if there was a telegram. What an appalling time, I must admit it! To avoid seeing Polya, Zinaida Fyodorovna dined and took tea in her room, and slept there too on a short curved sofa, tidying the bedclothes away herself. The first day or two I was the one that took telegrams, but when she received no reply she lost her trust in me and went to the telegraph office herself. Looking at her, I was impatient for a telegram to come too. I hoped he would invent some lie, make arrangements, for example, for her to be sent a telegram from some station or other. If he had got too involved in his cardgames, I thought, or had already managed to fall for another woman, then he would, of course, be reminded of us by both Gruzin and Kukushkin. But we waited in vain. Half-a-dozen times a day I went in to Zinaida Fyodorovna to tell her the whole truth, but she looked at me with the expression of a goat, her shoulders drooped, her lips shook, and I went away again without having said a word. Compassion and pity took away all my courage. Polya, cheerful and contented as if nothing had happened, tidied up the master's study, the bedroom, rummaged in the cupboards and rattled the crockery, and when going past Zinaida Fyodorovna's door she would hum a tune and cough. She was pleased to have someone hiding from her. In the evenings she went out, and at two or three o'clock rang on the doorbell and I would have to let her in and listen to remarks about my cough. Straight away another bell would be heard, I would run to the room next to the study, and Zinaida Fyodorovna, with her head poked around the door, would ask, 'Who was that ringing?' And she would be looking at my hands to see if they held a telegram.

When at last on Saturday there was a ring from downstairs and a familiar voice was heard on the staircase, she was so overjoyed that she burst into sobs; she rushed to meet him, hugged him and kissed his chest and sleeves while saying something unintelligible. The doorman brought in the suitcases, Polya's merry voice could be heard. It was just as if someone had arrived for the holidays!

'Why didn't you telegraph?' said Zinaida Fyodorovna, breathing hard from joy. 'Why? I wore myself out, I only just survived all this time... Oh God!'

'It's quite simple! On the very first day the senator and I went to Moscow and I didn't receive your telegrams,' said Orlov. 'After dinner, my sweet, I'll give you the most detailed report, but now I want to sleep, sleep and sleep... I'm exhausted after the train journey.'

It was clear that he had not slept all night: he had probably been playing cards and had a lot to drink. Zinaida Fyodorovna put him to bed, and after that we all walked about on tiptoe until evening. Dinner passed off perfectly well, but when they moved into the study for coffee, a serious conversation began. Zinaida Fyodorovna started to say something rapidly in a low tone; she spoke in French and sounded like a babbling brook, and then there was a loud sigh from Orlov and the sound of his voice.

'My God!' he said in French. 'Do you really have no fresher news than this old tune about the evil maid?'

'But dear, she robbed me and said a lot of insolent things to me.'

'But why doesn't she rob me and say insolent things to me? Why do I never notice maids, or janitors or menservants? My dear, you're simply being capricious and don't want to show any character... I even suspect you're pregnant. When I suggested to you that she be sacked, you demanded that she stay, and now you want me to sack her. But in cases like this I'm stubborn too: if you're wilful, then so am I. You want her to go, well, I want her to stay. This is the only way to cure your nerves.'

'Alright, that's enough!' said Zinaida Fyodorovna in fright. 'Let's stop talking about it... We'll leave it till tomorrow. Now tell me about Moscow... What's happening in Moscow?'

10

The next day – it was 7th January, St John the Baptist's day – after breakfast Orlov put on his black tailcoat and insignia to go and congratulate his father on his name-day. He needed to leave at two o'clock, but when he had finished dressing it was only half past one. How could he use the half hour? He walked around the sitting-room declaiming the congratulatory verse he used to recite for his father and mother when he was a child. Zinaida Fyodorovna was sitting there as well, ready to go to see her dressmaker or to the shops, and she listened to him with a smile. I do not know how the conversation started, but when I brought Orlov his gloves, he was standing in front of Zinaida Fyodorovna and saying to her with a wilful, plaintive look on his face:

'For God's sake, for the sake of all that is holy, do not talk about things that everybody already knows! And what is this unfortunate capacity of our clever, thinking ladies to talk with an air of profundity and fervour about things that set even a schoolboy's teeth on edge. Oh, if only you would exclude all these serious questions from your marriage programme! What a favour that would be!'

'We women shouldn't dare to judge for ourselves.'

'I give you complete freedom, be liberal and quote whatever writers you wish, but make one concession to me and don't discuss in my presence just two things: the pernicious nature of high society and the abnormalities of marriage. Try to understand, finally: high society is always criticised in order to contrast it with the society lived in by merchants, priests, petty bourgeois and peasants, all those Sidors and Nikitas. I find both societies offensive, but if I were offered the honest choice between the one and the other, then without hesitation I would choose high society, and this would not be falsehood or affectation, because all my tastes are on that side. Our society is both vulgar and hollow, but at least you and I speak decent French, read something now and again and don't whack one another in the guts, even when we have a major row, whereas with Sidor, Nikita and their like it's all, "we'll do the business", "straightways", "a curse on you", plus idolatry and the utterly unbridled morals of the drinking-house.'

'The peasant and the merchant feed you.'

'Yes, and so what? That puts not only me in a bad light, but them too. They feed me and kowtow before me, which means they don't have the intelligence or the honesty to behave differently. I'm not criticising or praising anyone, I just want to say this: the upper and the lower classes are no better than each other. In my heart and mind I am against them both, but my tastes are on the side of the former. Well now, where the abnormalities of marriage are concerned,' continued Orlov with a glance at the clock, 'it's time you realised that there are no abnormalities, there are for the time being just unclear demands on marriage. What do you want from marriage? In lawful and unlawful cohabitation, in all unions and cohab-itations, good and bad, the essence is one and the same. You ladies live for this essence alone, it is everything for you, without it your existence would have no meaning. You need nothing other than this essence, and so you take it, but ever since you read your fill of novellas, you've begun to feel ashamed of taking it, and you rush about from place to place, exchange men without a moment's thought, and to justify this chaos you've started talking of the abnormalities of marriage. Since you are neither able, nor willing to dismiss the essence, your chief enemy, your devil, since you continue to serve him slavishly, how can there be any serious conversations? Everything you say to me will be nonsense and affectation. I won't believe you.'

I went to find out from the doorman whether there was a cab, and when I returned I found a quarrel already under way. As sailors say, the wind was getting up.

'I can see that you want to shock me today with your cynicism,' said Zinaida Fyodorovna, walking around the sitting-room in great agitation. 'I feel disgusted listening to you. I am pure before God and man and I have no reason to repent. I left my husband for you and I'm proud of it. I'm proud, I swear it on my honour!'

'Well, splendid.'

'If you are an honest, decent man then you should be proud of what I have done as well. It raises me and you above the thousands of people who would like to do the same as I, but cannot bring themselves to do so because of a faint heart or petty calculation. But you aren't decent. You're afraid of freedom and jeer at an honest impulse out of fear that some ignoramus might suspect you of being an honest man. You're scared to show me to your acquaintances, there's no greater punishment for you than to drive down the street with me... What? Isn't it so? Why have you still not introduced me to your father and your cousin? Why? No, I'm sick of it all!' shouted Zinaida Fyodorovna, stamping her foot. 'I demand what is mine by right. Be so good as to introduce me to your father!'

'If you need him, then you can introduce yourself to him. He receives visitors every day in the morning from ten until half past.'

'How low you are!' said Zinaida Fyodorovna, wringing her hands in despair. 'Even if you're being insincere, just saying things you don't believe, for that bit of cruelty alone I could still hate you. Oh, how low you are!'

'We keep beating about the bush and never get round to talking about the real point. The whole point is that you were wrong and don't want to acknowledge it out loud. You imagined I was a hero and that I had some exceptional ideas and ideals, but then on checking it turned out that I was the most commonplace official, a card-player, and that I had no enthusiasm for any ideas. I am a worthy scion of that same rotten society from which you fled, horrified at its hollowness and vulgarity. Admit it and be fair: be indignant not with me, but with yourself, because it was you that was wrong, and not I.'

'Yes, I admit it: I was wrong!'

'Splendid. We've got to the point, thank God. Now listen a little more, if you want to. I cannot rise to your level, because I am too spoiled; you cannot descend to my level either, because you are too elevated. So only one thing remains...'

'What?' asked Zinaida Fyodorovna quickly with bated breath and turning suddenly white as a sheet.

'It remains to call logic to our assistance...'

'Georgy, why do you torment me?' said Zinaida Fyodorovna suddenly, and in Russian, with a break in her voice. 'Why? Understand my suffering...'

Orlov, frightened by her tears, went quickly to his study and – I do not know why: did he want to cause her more pain... or did he remember that this was the practice in such situations? – he locked the door behind him. She shrieked and chased after him with her dress swishing.

'What does this mean?' she asked, knocking on the door. 'What... what does this mean?' she repeated in a thin voice which broke off in indignation. 'Oh, so that's how it is? Well, know this: I hate and despise you! Everything is finished between us! Everything!'

Hysterical crying could be heard, mixed with loud laughter. In the drawing-room something small fell from a table and broke. Orlov slipped from the study into the hall by the other door and, glancing about him like a coward, quickly put on his greatcoat and top hat and went out.

Half an hour passed, then an hour, and still she cried. I remembered that she had no father, no mother, no relatives, that here she lived between a man who hated her and Polya, who was robbing her, and how cheerless her life appeared to me! I do not myself know why, but I went to her in the sitting-room. She, weak and helpless, with beautiful hair, who seemed to me a model of gentleness and elegance, was suffering as if she were sick; she lay on the couch, hiding her face, with her whole body shuddering.

'Madam, would you like me to go and fetch the doctor?' I asked quietly.

'No, there's no need... it's nothing,' she said and looked at me with tearstained eyes. 'My head aches a little... Thank you.'

I left the room. Then in the evening she wrote letter after letter and sent me first to Pekarsky, then to Kukushkin, then to Gruzin, and, finally, anywhere I chose, if only I would find Orlov quickly and give him the letter. Each time I came back again with the letter she told me off, implored, pushed money into my hand – as if in a fever. And that night she did not sleep, but sat in the drawing-room talking to herself.

The following day Orlov returned before dinner and they made it up.

The next Thursday after this Orlov complained to his friends about his unbearably difficult life; he smoked a lot and spoke with irritation:

'It's not life, it's the inquisition. Tears, shrieks, intelligent conversations, pleas for forgiveness, more tears and shrieks, and the sum of it all is – I no longer have my own flat, I've worn myself out and her too. Surely I won't have to live like this for another month or two? Surely not? But it's possible, you know!'

'Have a talk with her,' said Pekarsky.

'I've tried, but I can't. You can boldly tell any truth you like to an independent, reasoning person, but, I mean, here you are dealing with a creature that has neither will, nor character, nor logic. I cannot bear tears, they disarm me. When she cries I'm prepared to swear eternal love and cry myself.'

Pekarsky did not understand, scratched his broad forehead meditatively, and said, 'You really ought to rent a separate flat for her. I mean, it's so simple!'

'She needs me, not a flat. What's the point of talking?' sighed Orlov. 'I hear only endless conversations, but see no way out of my situation. I really am an innocent victim! I didn't make my bed, but I've got to lie on it. My whole life I refused to have anything to do with the role of a hero, I could never stand Turgenev's novels, and suddenly, as if part of a joke, I've become a real, genuine hero. I give my word of honour that I'm not a hero by any means, put forward irrefutable proof of it, but I'm not believed. Why am I not believed? I really must have something heroic in my physiognomy.'

'Go and inspect a province,' said Kukushkin, laughing.

'That's all that remains.'

A week after this conversation Orlov announced that he was again being sent away to work with the senator, and that same evening he left with his suitcases for Pekarsky's house.

11

On the threshold stood an elderly man of about sixty in a floor-length fur coat and a beaver-skin hat.

'Is Georgy Ivanych at home?' he asked.

At first I thought that this was one of the moneylenders, Gruzin's creditors, who sometimes came to Orlov for small sums of money, but when he entered the hall and undid his fur coat I saw the thick eyebrows and characteristically pursed lips which I had studied so well in photographs, and two rows of stars on his uniform tailcoat. I recognised him: this was Orlov's father, the famous statesman.

I replied that Georgy Ivanych was not at home. The old man pursed his lips tightly and looked to the side in indecision, presenting to me his dry, toothless profile.

'I shall leave a note,' he said. 'Show me the way.'

He left his overshoes in the hall and, without removing his long, heavy fur coat, went into the study. Here he sat down in the armchair in front of the desk and, before picking up the pen, he thought about something for three minutes or so, shading his eyes as if from the sun – in exactly the same way his son did when he was in a bad mood. His face was sad and pensive, with the expression of humility that I have only ever seen on the faces of the old and religious. I stood behind him, looking at his bald patch and the indentation on the back of his head, and it was clear as day to me that this weak, sick old man was now in my hands. For there was not a soul in the entire flat besides me and my enemy. I would only have to employ a little physical force, then rip off his watch to disguise my purpose and leave by the rear door, and I would have achieved immeasurably more than I could have expected when becoming a servant. I thought it unlikely that I would ever be presented with a better opportunity. But instead of acting, I looked with utter indifference first at his bald patch, then at his fur, and thought calmly about the relationship between this man and his only son and about how people who have been spoilt with wealth and power probably do not want to die...

'Have you worked for my son long?' he asked, carefully forming his large letters on the paper.

'More than two months, Your Supreme Excellency.'

He finished writing and stood up. I still had time. I hurried myself and clenched my fists in an attempt to squeeze out of my soul at least a drop of my former hatred; I remembered what a passionate, single-minded and tireless enemy I had been even so recently... But it is hard to strike a match against crumbling stone. His old, sad face and the cold sparkle of his stars aroused in me only trivial, cheap and irrelevant thoughts about the transience of all earthly things and imminent death...

'Goodbye, young fellow!' said the old man, putting on his hat, and left.

There was no possibility of further doubt: a change had taken place in me, I had become a different person. To test myself I started to recall the past, but I felt terrible straight away, as though I had looked accidentally into a dark, damp corner. I remembered my comrades and acquaintances, and my first thought was of how I would blush and be embarrassed now when I met any of them. For who was I now? What should I think about and do? Where should I go? What was I living for?

I did not understand a thing and was clearly conscious of one fact alone: I must pack my bags quickly and leave. Up until the old man's visit my being a servant still had some sense, but now it was just ridiculous. Tears dropped into my open suitcase, I was unbearably sad, but how I wanted to live! I was ready to embrace and fit into my short life everything a man can have. I wanted to talk and to read, to wield a hammer somewhere in a big factory, to stand watch and to guide a plough. I felt drawn to Nevsky Avenue, and to the fields, and to the sea – anywhere my imagination could manage. When Zinaida Fyodorovna returned I rushed to open the door and was particularly gentle in helping her off with her fur coat. For the last time!

Apart from the old man, we had two other visitors that day. In the evening, when it was already quite dark, Gruzin arrived unexpectedly to get some papers for Orlov. He opened the desk, took out the necessary papers and, rolling them into a tube, ordered me to put them in the hall next to his hat, while he himself went in to Zinaida Fyodorovna. She was lying on the sofa in the drawing-room with her head resting on her arms. Five or six days had already passed since Orlov had left on the inspection, and nobody knew when he would return, but she no longer sent any telegrams or expected any. Polya was still with us, but she did not seem to notice her. 'So be it!' was what I read on her impassive, very pale face. She, like Orlov, out of obstinacy now wanted to be unhappy; to spite herself and everything in the world she lay motionless on the sofa for days on end, wanting only the worst to happen to her, and expecting only the worst. She doubtless imagined to herself Orlov's return and the inevitable quarrels with him, then his growing coldness, betrayals, and then their parting, and these agonising thoughts perhaps gave her pleasure. But what would she say if she suddenly learned the real truth?

'I love you, godmother' said Gruzin, kissing her hand in greeting. 'You're so kind! And Georgey's gone away,' he lied. 'Gone away, the wicked fellow!'

He sat down with a sigh and gently stroked her hand.

'I'll sit here with you for an hour or so, if you don't mind, my dear,' he said. 'I don't feel like going home, and it's still too early to go to the Birshovs. The Birshovs are having a birthday party today for their Katya. She's a lovely little girl!'

I served him a glass of tea and a carafe of brandy. He evidently did not want the tea and drank it slowly. Handing me back the glass he asked timidly, 'I wonder, my friend, if you might find me something to eat? I've not had dinner yet.'

There was nothing in the flat. I went to a restaurant and brought him an ordinary one-rouble dinner.

'To your health, my dear!' he said to Zinaida Fyodorovna and drank a glass of vodka. 'My little one, your goddaughter, sends her love. Poor little thing, she's got scrofula! Ah, children, children!' he sighed. 'Say what you will, dear, it's nice to be a father. Georgey doesn't understand that feeling.'

He drank some more. Skinny, pale, with a napkin on his chest as if wearing a bib, he ate greedily and, raising his eyebrows, glanced guiltily by turns at Zinaida Fyodorovna and at me, like a little boy. If I had not given him his hazel-grouse or jelly, I think he would have cried. When his hunger was satisfied he became more cheerful and started to laugh and tell a story about the Birshovs, but noticing that it was uninteresting and Zinaida Fyodorovna was not laughing, he stopped. And somehow boredom suddenly set in. After dinner they both sat silent in the drawing-room in the light of just one lamp: he found it hard to lie, and she wanted to ask him about something, but could not bring herself to it. Half an hour or so passed like this. Gruzin looked at the clock.

'Well, I suppose it's time I went.'

'No, stay a little ... We need to have a talk.'

Again they fell silent. He sat down at the piano, touched one key, then began to play and quietly sing 'What does the coming day hold for me?', but, as usual, stopped straight away and shook his head.

'Play something,' requested Zinaida Fyodorovna.

'But what?' he asked with a shrug of the shoulders. 'I've already forgotten everything. I gave up long ago.'

Gazing at the ceiling, as if trying to remember, he played with wonderful expressiveness two pieces by Tchaikovsky, so warmly, so intelligently! His face was – as always – neither clever, nor foolish, and it seemed simply miraculous to me that a man I was used to seeing in the most mean and squalid setting was capable of such purity, of an upsurge of emotion so high and unattainable for me. Zinaida Fyodorovna flushed and began to walk around the drawing-room in agitation.

'Wait a moment, and if I can remember it, I'll play you a little something,' he said. 'I heard it played on the cello.'

Uncertainly and picking it out at first, and then with conviction he played 'The Swan' by Saint-Saëns. He played it through once and then once more.

'Nice, isn't it?' he said.

An agitated Zinaida Fyodorovna stopped beside him and asked, 'Tell me honestly, as a friend: what do you think of me?'

'What can I say?' he said, raising his eyebrows. 'I love you and think only good of you. But if you want me to say something in general on the question that interests you,' he continued, wiping the elbow of his sleeve and frowning, 'then, my dear, you know… Freely following the leanings of the heart doesn't always bring good people happiness. To feel free and at the same time happy, as it seems to me, you mustn't hide from yourself the fact that life is cruel, harsh and merciless in its conservatism, and you need to respond to it as it deserves; in other words, be just as it is, harsh and merciless in your striving for freedom. That's what I think.'

'How can I do that?' smiled Zinaida Fyodorovna sadly. 'I'm already exhausted. I'm so exhausted, I won't lift a finger for my own salvation.'

'Get ye to a nunnery[6].'

This was meant as a joke, but after his words tears began to shine in Zinaida Fyodorovna's eyes and then in his own.

'Well, ma'am,' he said, 'we've sat long enough, off we go. Goodbye, my dear. May God grant you health.'

He kissed both her hands, gently stroked them and said he would come again without fail in a day or two. In the hall, while putting on the coat like a child's dressing-gown, he rummaged for a long time in his pockets to give me a tip, but could not find any money.

'Goodbye, my dear chap!' he said sadly and went.

I shall never forget the atmosphere left behind by that man. Zinaida Fyodorovna still carried on walking around the drawing-room in agitation. She was not lying down, but walking – that in itself was a good thing. I wanted to exploit the atmosphere to have a frank talk with her and then leave immediately, but scarcely had I managed to see Gruzin off before the bell rang. It was Kukushkin.

'Is Georgy Ivanych at home?' he asked. 'Has he returned? No, you tell me? What a shame! In that case, I'll go and kiss the mistress' hand and then be off. Zinaida Fyodorovna, may I?' he shouted. 'I want to kiss your hand. I'm sorry I'm here so late.'

He did not stay in the drawing-room for long, no more than ten minutes, but it seemed to me as if he had been sitting there for an age and would never leave. I bit my lips in indignation and annoyance and now hated Zinaida Fyodorovna. 'Why doesn't she get rid of him?' I thought in exasperation, although it was obvious that he bored her.

While I was helping him on with his fur coat, as a mark of his particularly good disposition towards me he asked how it was that I managed without a wife.

'But I don't suppose you miss a trick,' he said, laughing. 'I expect you and Polya get up to some hanky-panky... You naughty fellow!'

Despite my experience of life, I knew little of people at that time, and it is quite possible that I often exaggerated what was insignificant and completely failed to notice what was important. It occurred to me that Kukushkin was not tittering and flattering me for nothing: did he not hope that I, as a servant, would chatter in all the servants' halls and kitchens about how he visited us in the evenings when Orlov was not at home and sat with Zinaida Fyodorovna until late at night? And when my gossip reached the ears of his acquaintances, he would lower his eyes in confusion and wag his little finger. And, I thought, looking at his little honeyed face, would he himself not pretend, and perhaps let slip over cards this very day, that he had already won Zinaida Fyodorovna from Orlov?

The hatred which was so lacking at midday when the old man had come now took control of me. Kukushkin finally left and, listening to the shuffling of his leather overshoes, I felt a strong desire to send after him some vulgar abuse in farewell, but I resisted. Yet when his steps fell quiet on the staircase I went back into the hall and, without knowing what I was doing myself, I grabbed the bundle of papers that Gruzin had forgotten and ran headlong down the stairs. Coatless and hatless I ran out into the street. It was not cold, but large snowflakes were falling and the wind was blowing.

'Your Excellency!' I cried, chasing after Kukushkin. 'Your Excellency!' He stopped by a street lamp and looked round in bewilderment. 'Your Excellency!' I panted. 'Your Excellency!'

And as I had not thought what to say, I struck him a couple of times across the face with the bundle of papers. Completely uncomprehending and not even surprised – to such a degree had I stunned him – he leant back on the lamp-post and covered his face with his arms. At that moment an army doctor was walking past and saw me hitting a man, but he only looked at us in bewilderment and went on his way.

I began to feel ashamed and ran back into the house.

12

Out of breath and with my head wet from the snow, I ran into the servants' hall and immediately threw off my tailcoat, put on my jacket and overcoat and carried my suitcase out into the hallway. Escape! But before leaving I sat down quickly and started writing to Orlov:

'I am leaving you my fake passport,' I began, 'please keep it as a memento, you fake of a man, Mr St Petersburg official!

'Slipping into a home under an assumed name, observing intimate life from beneath a servant's mask, seeing and hearing everything with a view to revealing falsehood unbidden later on – all this, you will say, smacks of thieving. Yes, but I cannot be bothered with nobility now. I have lived through dozens of your dinners and suppers when you talked and did as you pleased, while I had to listen, observe and remain silent – I do not want to make you a gift of that. What is more, if there is no living soul near you who might dare to tell you the truth without flattery, then at least let the manservant Stepan reveal the true magnificence of your physiognomy.'

I was not pleased with this opening, but I did not feel like altering it. And did it really matter?

The large windows with their dark curtains, the bed, the crumpled tailcoat on the floor and the wet marks from my feet looked stern and sad. And there was a special sort of silence.

Probably because I had rushed out into the street without a hat or overshoes, I had run up a high fever. My face was burning, my legs were aching... My heavy head was bending towards the table, and my thoughts seemed somehow split in two, as if every thought was being followed in my brain by its shadow.

'I am sick, weak, morally depressed,' I continued, 'and I cannot write to you as I would wish. To begin with I had a strong desire to insult and humiliate you, but now I feel that I do not have the right to do so. You and I have both fallen, and neither of us will ever rise again, and my letter, even if it were eloquent, powerful and frightening, would nevertheless be like knocking on the lid of a coffin: knock as much as you like, you won't wake him! No exertions could ever warm up your damned cold blood now, and you know that better than I. Why write then? But my head and heart are burning, I carry on writing and am agitated for some reason, as if this letter might yet save us both. Because of my fever the thoughts in my head do not tie up, and the pen scratches across the paper senselessly somehow, but the question I want to ask you stands clearly before me as if written in fire.

'Why I weakened and fell prematurely is not hard to explain. Like the strong man in the Bible I took up the gates of Gaza to carry them to the top of the hill; only when I grew tired, when my youth and health were extinguished forever, I noticed that these gates were too much for my shoulders and that I had deceived myself. What is more, I was in constant, cruel pain. I experienced hunger, cold, sickness, loss of freedom: I did not and do not know personal happiness, I have no shelter, my memories are bad and my conscience often fears them. But why did you fall, you? What fateful, devilish causes prevented your life from opening into the full flower of spring? Why did you, before you had yet had time to start to live, hurry to throw off the image and likeness of God and turn into a cowardly animal that barks because it is itself afraid, and in barking frightens others? You are afraid of life, afraid, like an Asiatic, one who sits for days on the end on a feather bed smoking a hookah. Yes, you read a lot, and a European tailcoat sits well on you, but nevertheless, with what tenderness, the purely Asiatic solicitude of a khan, do you protect yourself from hunger, cold, physical strain – pain and anxiety. How early did your spirit hide inside an eastern robe; what a coward you played in the face of real life and nature with which every healthy and normal man does battle. How soft, cosy, warm and comfortable things are for you – and how dull! Yes, it can be deadly dull with no hope of relief, as in solitary confinement, but you try to hide from that enemy too: for eight hours a day you play cards.

'And your irony? Oh, how well I understand it! Free, living, energetic thought is inquisitive and masterful; for a lazy, idle mind it is intolerable. So that it did not disturb your peace, you, like thousands of your peers, hastened from your early days to keep it within bounds; you armed yourself with an ironic attitude to life, or call it what you will, and constrained, intimidated thought does not dare jump over the fence you erected for it, and when you mock ideas which are *all* allegedly familiar to you, then you resemble a deserter, who ignominiously flees the battlefield, but, to deaden his shame, jeers at war and bravery. Cynicism deadens pain. In some story by Dostoevsky[7] an old man tramples the portrait of his beloved daughter underfoot because he has wronged her, while you laugh nastily and vulgarly at ideas of goodness and truth, because you no longer have the power to return to them. Every sincere and truthful hint at your fall is terrible for you, and you surround yourself intentionally only with those who know how to flatter your weaknesses. And not without reason, not without reason are you so afraid of tears!

'Incidentally, your attitude to women… Shamelessness we inherited with our flesh and blood and in shamelessness are we raised, but the reason we are men is that we can try to overcome the beast in us. With maturity, when *all* ideas had become familiar to you, you could not help but see the truth; you knew it, yet you did not follow it, you were frightened by it and, in order to deceive your conscience, you began assuring yourself loudly that it was not you that was guilty, but women themselves, that they were just as base as your attitude to them. Cold, crude jokes, braying laughter, all your countless theories about an essence, about unclear demands on marriage, about the ten sous paid to a woman by a French workman, your eternal references to female logic, mendacity, weakness and so on – does all this not seem like a desire at any cost to bend women so low towards the dirt that they and your attitude to them are on the same level? You are a weak, unhappy, unattractive man.'

In the drawing-room Zinaida Fyodorovna started playing the piano, trying to remember the piece by Saint-Saëns that Gruzin had played. I went and lay down on the bed, but, remembering that it was time I left, I made myself get up and with a heavy, burning head I went back to the table.

'But here is the question,' I continued. 'Why are we exhausted? Why do we, at first so passionate, bold, noble, full of belief, why do we become, by the age of thirty or thirty-five, completely bankrupt? Why does one fade away with consumption, a second put a bullet through his forehead, a third seek oblivion in vodka and cards, a fourth, to deaden his fear and anguish, cynically trample underfoot the portrait of his pure, fine youth? Why do we, once fallen, no longer attempt to rise, and, when we lose one thing, why do we not seek another? Why?

'The thief hanging on his cross managed to regain the joy of life and a bold, realisable hope, although he had perhaps not more than an hour left to live. You still have many long years before you, and even I shall probably not die as soon as one might think. What if by a miracle the present turned out to be a dream, a terrible nightmare, and we woke up renewed, pure, strong, proud of our truth?... Sweet dreams burn me and I can scarcely breathe in my agitation. I want to live so much, I want our life to be sacred, elevated and grand like the vault of heaven. We will live! The sun does not rise twice in one day and life is not granted twice – so take a tight hold on the remains of your life and save them...'

I did not write a single word more. There were many thoughts in my head, but they were all vague and diffused and would not fall into line. Without concluding the letter, I wrote beneath it my title, first name and surname and went into the study. It was dark. I groped for the desk and put the letter down. In the darkness I must have bumped into some furniture and made a noise.

'Who's there?' came an alarmed voice from the drawing-room.

And immediately the clock on the desk gently struck one.

13

I scratched at the door as I fumbled for it in the darkness for at least half a minute or so, then I slowly opened it and went into the drawing-room. Zinaida Fyodorovna was lying on the couch and, raising herself onto one elbow, she gazed in my direction. I could not bring myself to speak, and walked slowly past her as she followed me with her eyes. I stood a little while in the reception hall, then walked past her again, and she looked at me closely, in bewilderment and even in fear. Finally I halted and made myself say, 'He isn't coming back!'

She got up quickly and looked at me in puzzlement.

'He isn't coming back!' I repeated, and my heart began beating wildly. 'He isn't coming back, because he never left St Petersburg. He's staying with Pekarsky.'

She understood and believed me – I could see it from her instant pallor and from the way she suddenly crossed her arms at her breast in fear and supplication. In a moment her recent past flashed by in her memory, she grasped it and saw the whole truth with implacable clarity. But at the same time she remembered that I was a servant, an inferior being... A scoundrel with rumpled hair, with a face red from fever, drunk perhaps, dressed in some common overcoat, had rudely intruded on her private life, and this insulted her. Sternly she said to me, 'Nobody is asking you. Get out of here.'

'Oh, believe me!' I said excitedly, stretching my arms out to her. 'I am no servant, I am just as free as you!'

I told her my name and very, very quickly, so that she did not interrupt me or go to her room, I explained who I was and why I was living there. This new discovery shocked her more than the first. Previously she still had some hope that the servant had lied, or was mistaken, or had talked nonsense, but now, after my confession, there remained no doubt in her mind. From the expression of her unhappy eyes and face, which had aged, lost its softness and suddenly become unattractive, I could see that she found this unbearably hard, that it had not been a good thing to start the conversation; but I continued excitedly, 'The senator and the inspection were invented to deceive you. In January, just as now, he didn't go away anywhere, but stayed with Pekarsky, and I met with him every day and took part in the deceit. You were a burden, your presence here was hated, you were laughed at... If you could have eavesdropped on him and his friends here mocking you and your love, then you wouldn't have stayed for a single minute! Run away from here! Run away!'

'Well?' she said in a trembling voice and ran her hand across her hair. 'Well? So be it.'

Her eyes were full of tears, her lips trembled, and her whole face was amazingly pale and breathed fury. Orlov's mean, petty falsehood enraged her and seemed to her contemptible and ridiculous; she smiled, and I did not like this smile of hers.

'Well?' she repeated and again ran her hand across her hair. 'So be it. He imagines I'll die from humiliation, but I find it...

funny. He's hiding for nothing.' She moved away from the piano and said with a shrug, 'For nothing... It would be simpler to have it out with me rather than hiding and moving around other people's flats. I have eyes, I could see it myself long ago... and I was just waiting for his return to have it out with him once and for all.'

Then she sat down in the armchair by the table and, lowering her head onto the arm of the sofa, she began to cry bitterly. Only one candle was burning in the candelabrum in the drawing-room, and it was dark where she was sitting, but I could see her head and shoulders shuddering, and her hair coming loose and covering her neck, face and hands... In her quiet, steady crying – not the usual hysterical crying of a woman – could be heard insult, humiliated pride, hurt, and something interminable and hopeless which cannot be got used to and which can no longer be put right. In my agitated, suffering soul her crying found an echo; I had already forgotten about my illness and everything else, and I walked around the drawing-room, muttering in dismay, 'What sort of life is this?... Oh, you can't live like this! You can't! It's... madness, a crime, not life!'

'What humiliation!' she said through her sobs. 'To live together... to smile at me when I'm a burden to him, ridiculous... Oh, what humiliation!'

She raised her head and, gazing at me with tearstained eyes through hair wet with tears, and trying to put in place this hair that made looking at me difficult, she asked, 'And they laughed?'

'Those men found you funny, and your love, and Turgenev, of whom you have apparently read too much. And if we both die now of despair, then they'll find that funny too. They'll make up a funny story and tell it at your funeral mass. But why

71

talk about them?' I said impatiently. 'We must escape from here. I can't stay here a minute longer.'

She started crying again. I moved away to the piano and sat down.

'What are we waiting for?' I asked gloomily. 'It's already after two.'

'I'm not waiting for anything,' she said. 'I'm lost.'

'Why talk like that? We'd do better to think together about what we should do. Neither you nor I can stay here any longer... Where do you intend to go from here?'

Suddenly the bell in the hall rang. My heart sank. Could it be Orlov, had Kukushkin complained to him about me? What would we do on meeting? I went to open the door. It was Polya. She walked in, shook the snow off her hooded cape in the hall, and, without saying a word to me, went off to her room. When I returned to the drawing-room, Zinaida Fyodorovna, pale as a dead man, was standing in the middle of the room and looking towards me with eyes open wide.

'Who was that coming in?' she asked softly.

'Polya,' I replied.

She ran her hand across her hair and closed her eyes in exhaustion.

'I shall leave here now,' she said. 'Be so kind as to accompany me across the Neva. What's the time now?'

'A quarter to three.'

14

When a little later we left the house, the street was dark and deserted. Wet snow was falling and a moist wind lashed at our faces. As I recall, it was then the beginning of March, there was a thaw, and for several days the cabs had been on wheels. Upset by going down the back stairs, by the cold, the dark of the night and the janitor in his sheepskin who had questioned us before letting us through the gate, Zinaida Fyodorovna was much weakened and low in spirits. When we had got into a cab and put the top up, with her whole body trembling she began speaking hurriedly of how grateful she was to me.

'I don't doubt your goodwill, but I'm embarrassed that you're taking such trouble…' she mumbled. 'Oh, I understand, I understand… When Gruzin was there today, I sensed that he was lying and hiding something. Well? So be it. But all the same, I feel guilty about your taking such trouble.'

She still had doubts. To dispel them completely I ordered the cab driver to go along Sergiyevskaya Street; stopping him by Pekarsky's door, I got out of the cab and rang the bell. When the doorman came out, I asked him loudly, so that Zinaida Fyodorovna could hear, whether Georgy Ivanych was in.

'In,' he replied. 'Arrived about half an hour ago. Probably asleep already. What do you want, then?'

Zinaida Fyodorovna could not restrain herself and leaned out of the cab.

'And has Georgy Ivanych been staying here long?' she asked.

'Two weeks or more.'

'And hasn't been away anywhere?'

'Nowhere,' answered the doorman and looked at me in surprise.

'Let him know early tomorrow,' I said, 'that his sister has come to visit him from Warsaw. Goodbye.'

After that we rode on. There was no apron in the cab, the flakes of snow fell on us and the wind, especially on the Neva,

73

penetrated to the bones. I began to feel that we had been driving a long time, suffering a long time, and that I had long been able to hear Zinaida Fyodorovna's unsteady breathing. Fleetingly, in a state of near delirium, as if falling asleep, I looked back on my strange, incoherent life, and for some reason the melodrama 'The Beggars of Paris',[8] which I saw once or twice as a child, came to mind. And for some reason, when, to shake myself out of this near delirium, I looked out from under the hood and saw the dawn, all the images from the past, all my indistinct thoughts merged within me into one powerful idea: Zinaida Fyodorovna and I were already irrevocably lost. This was a certainty, as if the cold blue sky held a prophecy, but a moment later I was already thinking of something else and believing something else.

'What will become of me now?' said Zinaida Fyodorovna in a voice hoarse from the cold and damp. 'Where shall I go, what shall I do? Gruzin said: get ye to a nunnery. Oh, I would go! I would change my clothes, my face, name, thoughts... everything, everything, and would hide myself away forever. But I won't be allowed into a nunnery. I'm pregnant.'

'We'll go abroad together tomorrow,' I said.

'It's not possible. My husband won't let me have a passport.'

'I'll get you out without a passport.'

The cab stopped beside a two-storeyed wooden house, painted a dark colour. I rang the bell. Taking from me a small, light basket, the only luggage we had brought with us, Zinaida Fyodorovna gave me a rather sour smile and said, 'These are my *bijoux*...'

But she had become so weak that she did not have the strength to hold these *bijoux*. We waited a long time for the door to be opened. After the third or fourth ring a light flashed in the windows, and footsteps, coughing and whispering could be heard; at last the lock clicked, and in the doorway there appeared a plump serving-woman with a red, frightened face. A certain distance behind her stood a small, thin old woman with cropped grey hair, wearing a white nightshirt and holding a candle. Zinaida Fyodorovna ran inside and threw herself onto the neck of this old woman.

'Nina, I've been deceived!' she sobbed loudly. 'I've been crudely, horribly deceived! Nina! Nina!'

I handed the basket to the serving-woman. The door was locked, but the sobbing and cries of 'Nina!' were still audible. I got into the cab and ordered the driver to drive slowly to Nevsky Avenue. I needed to think of where I too was to rest that night.

The next day towards evening I was with Zinaida Fyodorovna. She had altered greatly. On her pale, much thinner face there was no longer any trace of tears, and the expression was different. I do not know if it was because I saw her now in another setting, far from luxurious, and because our relationship had changed, or perhaps great grief had already left its mark on her, but she did not seem to me now so elegant and well-dressed; her figure seemed to have become smaller, in her movements, in her walk, in her face I noticed an excessive nervousness, impulsiveness, as though she were in a hurry, and the former softness was gone even from her smile. I was now dressed in an expensive suit which I had bought myself that afternoon. First of all she examined this suit and the hat in my hand, then rested her impatient, searching gaze on my face, as though studying it.

'Your transformation still seems some kind of miracle to me,' she said. 'Excuse me, I'm inspecting you with such curiosity. But then you are an extraordinary man.'

I told her once more who I was and why I had been living with Orlov, I talked about it for longer and in more detail than the day before. She listened very attentively and, without letting me finish, said, 'Everything's finished for me there. You know, I couldn't restrain myself and I wrote a letter. Here's the reply.'

On the sheet she passed to me in Orlov's hand was written: 'I am not going to try and justify myself. But you must agree: you were wrong, not I. I wish you happiness and beg you soon to forget your respectful G. O.

'P. S. I'm sending your things.'

The chests and baskets sent by Orlov were standing there in the sitting-room, and among them was my sorry little suitcase as well.

'So…' said Zinaida Fyodorovna, but did not finish.

We were silent for a while. She took the note and held it for a minute or two in front of her eyes, and during this time her face took on that same haughty, contemptuous and proud, hard expression which she had had the previous day at the start of our talk; tears came into her eyes, not timid, not bitter, but proud, angry tears.

'Listen,' she said, getting up impulsively and moving away to the window so that I could not see her face. 'This is what I've decided: tomorrow I shall go abroad with you.'

'Splendid. I'm ready to go today if you like.'

'Recruit me. Have you read Balzac?' she asked suddenly, turning round. 'Have you? His novel *Old Goriot* ends with the hero looking at Paris from the top of a hill and threatening the city: "Now we settle accounts!" and after that he begins a new life. I'll do the same, when I look at St Petersburg for the last time from the train carriage, I'll say to it: "Now we settle accounts!"'

And, saying this, she smiled at her joke, but for some reason her whole body shuddered.

15

In Venice I began to suffer the pains of pleurisy. I probably caught cold on the evening when we went by boat from the station to the Hotel Bauer. I was obliged to take to my bed from the very first day and stay there for some two weeks. Every morning while I was ill Zinaida Fyodorovna came from her room to mine to drink coffee with me, and then she read aloud to me from the French and Russian books of which we had bought a large number in Vienna. I had already known these books for a long time, or else they were of no interest to me, but a sweet, kind voice rang out beside me so that the content of all of them boiled down essentially to one thing: I was not alone. She would go off for a walk, return in her pale grey dress and light straw hat, cheerful, warmed by the spring sunshine, and, sitting down by my bed and bending low towards my face, she would recount something about Venice or read the books – and I felt content.

At night I was cold, in pain and bored, but during the daytime I was intoxicated by life – you could not think of a better expression. The bright, hot sun beating in at the open windows and the door onto the balcony, the shouts from below, the splashing of oars, the ringing of bells, the rolling thunder of the cannon at noon and the sense of complete, complete freedom worked wonders with me; on my sides I could feel powerful, broad wings, which carried me away God knows where. And what delight, how much joy at times from the thought that now another life was moving along beside mine, that I was the servant, the watchman, the friend, the indispensable companion of a creature young, beautiful and rich, but weak, injured and alone! Even being unwell is pleasant when you know that there are people who await your recovery like a holiday. Once I heard her whispering outside the door with my doctor, and then she came in to me with tear-stained eyes; that was a bad sign, but I was touched and my heart felt unusually light.

Later I was permitted to go out onto the balcony. The sun and a light breeze from the sea soothe and caress my sick body. I look down at the long-familiar gondolas which float with feminine grace, smoothly and majestically, as though they are alive, and sense all the splendour of this unique and charming culture. There is the smell of the sea. Somewhere stringed instruments are being played and two voices are singing. How lovely! How unlike that night in St Petersburg when wet snow was falling and beating so rudely in our faces! If you look up straight across the canal, the seashore is visible, and on the open sea on the horizon the sun ripples across the water so brightly that it is painful to watch. My soul is drawn that way, to the dear, good sea to which I gave my youth. I want to live! To live – and nothing else!

After two weeks I began going out wherever I wanted. I liked to sit in the sun listening to a gondolier without under-standing and looking for hours on end at the little house where, they say, Desdemona lived – a naive, sad little house with a virginal expression, light as lace, so light, it seemed as if you could set it moving with one hand. I stood for long periods at the grave of Canova and could not tear my gaze from the sorrowful lion. And in the Palace of the Doges I was always drawn to the same corner, where the unfortunate Marino Faliero was daubed with black paint. How fine to be an artist, a poet, a dramatist, I thought, but if that is unattainable for me, then at least I could go in for mysticism! Ah, to add just a little faith of some sort to this serene calm and satisfaction filling my soul.

In the evening we ate oysters, drank wine, went for rides. I remember our black gondola quietly rocking on the spot, beneath it the scarcely audible lapping of the water. Trembling and flickering here and there are the reflections of the stars and the lights along the shore. Not far from us in a gondola hung with coloured lanterns which reflect in the water, some people are sitting and singing. The sound of guitars, violins, mandolins, male and female voices rings out in the darkness, and Zinaida Fyodorovna, pale, with a serious, almost stern face, sits alongside me with her teeth and fists tightly clenched. She is thinking of something, does not move so much as an eyebrow and does not hear me. Her face, pose, and immobile, expressionless gaze, and incredibly gloomy, terrible memories, cold as snow, while all around – gondolas, lights, music, a song with the energetic, passionate cry, '*Jammo!... Jam-mo!...*' – what contrasts there are in life! When she sat like this with her fists clenched, like stone, grieving, it seemed to me that we were both protagonists in some old-fashioned novel entitled 'The Ill-fated Lady' or 'The Abandoned Woman' or something of the sort. Both of us: she was the ill-fated, deserted woman, and I was the true, devoted friend, the dreamer, and, if you like, the superfluous man, the failure, no longer capable of anything but coughing and dreaming, and, perhaps, sacrificing himself as well... but who and what needed my sacrifices now? And the question arose, what was I to sacrifice?

After our evening outing we always had tea and talked in her room. We were not afraid of touching old wounds that had not yet healed, on the contrary, for some reason I even experienced pleasure when telling her about my life with Orlov or candidly mentioning the relations which I knew about and could not have been concealed from me.

'There were moments when I hated you,' I said. 'When he was being wilful, condescending and lying, I was astonished, how was it that you saw and understood nothing, when everything was so clear. You kiss his hands, kneel, flatter...'

'When I... kissed his hands and knelt, I was in love,' she said, blushing.

'Was it really so difficult to work him out? What a fine sphinx! A Gentleman of the Bedchamber and a sphinx! I'm not reproaching you with anything, God forbid!' I continued, feeling that I was a little rough, that I had no social graces and none of the delicacy which is so necessary when you are dealing with somebody else's soul; previously, before I met her, I had not noticed this shortcoming in myself. 'But how could you not guess?' I repeated, though this time more quietly and uncertainly.

'You mean you despise my past, and you're right,' she said in great agitation. 'You belong to a special category of people who cannot be measured with the usual yardstick, your moral demands are exceptionally severe and, I understand, you cannot forgive; I understand you, and if I contradict sometimes, it doesn't mean that I look upon things differently to you; I talk my former nonsense simply because I haven't yet had time to wear out my old dresses and prejudices. I myself hate and despise my past, and Orlov, and my love... What sort of love was it? Now all that even seems ridiculous,' she said, going up to the window and looking down at the canal. 'All these loves only cloud your conscience and confuse you. The meaning of life is in one thing alone – in struggle. To put your heel on the vile head of the snake so that it cracks open! That's where the meaning is. In that alone, or else there is no meaning at all.'

I told her long stories from my past and described my truly amazing escapades. But of the change that had taken place in me I let slip not a word. She always listened to me very attentively and at the interesting points rubbed her hands as if in annoyance that she had not yet been able to experience such adventures, terrors and joys, but suddenly she would fall into thought, retreat into herself and I could tell from her face that she was no longer listening to me.

I shut the windows overlooking the canal and asked whether I should stoke up the fire.

'No, there's no need. I'm not cold,' she said, smiling listlessly, 'I've just gone all weak. You know, it seems to me that recently I've become dreadfully clever. I have extraordinary, original thoughts now. When I think about the past, for example, about my life then... well, about people generally, everything merges into one thing – the image of my stepmother. Rude, brazen, soulless, false, debauched, and, on top of all that, a morphine addict. My father, weak and spineless, married my mother for her money and drove her to consumption, but this second wife of his, my stepmother, he loved her passionately, madly... The things I've endured! But why talk about it? Anyway, everything, as I say, merges into the one image... And it's annoying: why did my stepmother die? I'd like to meet her now!'

'Why?'

'Well, I don't know...' she replied, laughing and shaking her head prettily. 'Goodnight. Get well. As soon as you're better, we'll start on our work... It's high time.'

When I took hold of the door handle, having already said

goodnight, she said, 'What do you think? Is Polya still with him?'

'Probably.'

And I went to my room. We lived like this for a whole month. One overcast day, when we were standing together by the window in my room and gazing silently at the clouds moving in from the sea and the dark blue canal, expecting it to pour down at any moment, and when a narrow, dense band of rain had covered the seashore like gauze, we both suddenly felt bored. That same day we left for Florence.

16

It happened in the autumn in Nice. One morning when I went into her hotel room she was sitting in an armchair with her legs crossed, hunched up, drawn, with her hands over her face, sobbing bitterly, and her long hair hung loose onto her knees. The impression of the wonderful, astonishing sea that I had just seen and of which I wanted to tell her suddenly left me and my heart contracted in pain.

'What's wrong?' I asked; she took one hand away from her face and waved for me to leave the room. 'But what's wrong?' I repeated, and for the first time since we had met I kissed her hand.

'No, no, it's nothing!' she said quickly. 'Oh, it's nothing, nothing... Go away... You can see I'm not dressed.'

I went out in terrible confusion. The calm and the carefree mood that I had known for so long were poisoned by compassion. I longed passionately to fall at her feet, beg her not to cry in isolation, but to share her grief with me, and the steady roar of the sea now began to growl in my ears like a gloomy prophecy, and I could see in the future fresh tears, fresh sorrows and losses. What, oh what was she crying about? – I asked, recalling her face and air of suffering. I remembered that she was pregnant. She tried to conceal her condition both from other people and from herself. Indoors she wore a loose-fitting smock or a blouse with exaggeratedly deep tucks at the breast, and when she went out anywhere she would lace her corset so tight that twice she fainted while I was walking with her. She never spoke to me about her pregnancy, and once, when I suggested in passing that it would do her no harm to consult a doctor, she turned quite red and said not a word.

When I went in to her later on she was already dressed with her hair in place.

'There, there!' I said, seeing that she was again on the point of tears. 'Let's go down to the sea instead and have a chat.'

'I can't talk. Forgive me, but I'm in the sort of mood now when you want to be alone. And, Vladimir Ivanovich, when you wish to enter my room another time, please knock on the door beforehand.'

This 'beforehand' somehow had a particular, unfeminine ring. I went out. The damned St Petersburg mood was returning, and all my dreams curled up and shrank like leaves in the heat. I felt that I was alone again, that there was no intimacy between us. I was for her the same as a spider's web is for this palm tree here, a web suspended on it by chance and which would be torn off and carried away by the wind. I strolled in the square where music was playing, dropped into the casino; there I cast an eye over the women, dressed to kill and heavily scented, and each of them glanced at me as if to say, 'You're on your own, splendid...' Later I went out onto the terrace and gazed at the sea for a long time.

On the distant horizon not a single sail, on the shore to the left in a purplish haze – mountains, gardens, towers, houses, and the sun playing on everything; but everything is foreign, indifferent, what a mess…

17

She came to my room in the mornings to drink coffee as before, but we no longer had dinner together; she did not feel like eating, as she put it, and her nourishment consisted only of coffee, tea and various little snacks like oranges and caramels.

And we no longer had any conversations in the evenings. I do not know why it was so. After I had found her in tears she began to treat me lightly somehow, at times carelessly, even with irony, and for some reason she called me 'my good sir'. What had previously seemed to her frightening, amazing and heroic and had aroused envy and delight in her now touched her not one bit, and after hearing me out she would normally stretch a little and say, 'Yes, we've all heard of the Battle of Poltava, my good sir.'

It was sometimes even the case that I did not meet with her for days on end. You could knock timidly and guiltily at her door – no reply; you would knock again – silence… You would stand by the door and listen; and then a chambermaid walks past and announces coldly, '*Madame est partie*'. And after that you walk up and down the hotel corridor, up and down, up and down… English people of some sort, buxom ladies, waiters in tailcoats… And as I gaze for some time at the long striped carpet which runs the length of the corridor, it comes into my mind that I am playing a strange and

84

probably false role in this woman's life and that it is no longer in my power to change this role; I run to my room, fall onto the bed and think and think, but I come up with nothing, and it is clear to me only that I want to live, and that the plainer, drier and harder her face becomes, the closer she is to me and the stronger and more painful is my sense of our kinship. Let me be 'my good sir', let there be the light, disdainful tone, anything at all, only do not leave me, my treasure. I am frightened now of being alone.

Later I go back out into the corridor and listen closely in alarm... I have no dinner and do not notice the evening coming on. Finally, after ten o'clock, familiar footsteps are heard and Zinaida Fyodorovna appears at the turning by the staircase.

'Taking a walk?' she asks as she passes. 'It would be better to go outside... Goodnight!'

'Aren't we going to see one another today then?'

'It's already late, I think. But as you wish.'

'Tell me, where have you been?' I ask, following her into the room.

'Where? Monte Carlo.' She takes from her pocket a dozen or so gold coins and says, 'There, my good sir, I won. At roulette.'

'You're no gambler.'

'Why not? I'm going again tomorrow.'

I imagined her with her sick, unhealthy look, pregnant and tightly corseted, standing by the gaming table in a crowd of cocottes, senile old women swarming around gold like flies around honey, and I remembered that she had gone to Monte Carlo without telling me for some reason...

'I don't believe you,' I said once. 'You wouldn't go there.'

'Don't worry. I can't lose a lot.'

'It's not a question of losing,' I said in annoyance. 'Did it really not occur to you while you were playing, that the glitter of gold, all these women, old and young, the croupiers, the entire setting, that all this is a base, vile mockery of the labour of the working man, of blood and sweat?'

'If you don't gamble, then what is there to do here?' she asked. 'And as for the labour of the working man and blood and sweat – keep the eloquence for another time. But now, as you've started, allow me to continue; allow me to put the question bluntly: what am I to do here and what am I to do in the future?'

'What's to be done?' I said with a shrug. 'That question can't be answered straight away.'

'I'm asking you for an honest answer, Vladimir Ivanych,' she said, and her face became angry. 'Since I've gone so far as to ask you this question, it's not to hear platitudes. I'm asking you,' she continued, striking the palm of her hand on the table as though beating time, 'what should I be doing here? And not only here, in Nice, but in general?'

I was silent and looked out of the window at the sea. My heart began beating dreadfully.

'Vladimir Ivanych,' she said softly, gasping for breath; it was hard for her to speak. 'Vladimir Ivanych, if you don't believe in the cause yourself, if you're no longer thinking of returning to it, then why… why did you drag me here from St Petersburg? Why did you make promises and rouse mad hopes in me? Your convictions have altered, you've become a different man, and nobody can reproach you for that – our convictions aren't always within our power, but … but Vladimir Ivanych, for God's sake, why are you dishonest,' she continued quietly, coming up to me. 'When all these months I dreamed out loud, raved, got carried away by my plans,

86

rebuilt my life in a new way, why did you not then tell me the truth, instead of keeping silent or encouraging me with stories and behaving as if you were in complete sympathy with me? Why? What made that necessary?'

'It's difficult to admit your own bankruptcy,' I said, turning, but not looking at her. 'No, I've lost faith, I'm weary, my spirits are low… It's hard to be honest, terribly hard, and I was silent. God forbid that anyone should go through what I have.'

I thought I was about to burst out crying, so I fell silent.

'Vladimir Ivanych,' she said, taking both my hands in hers. 'You've been through and experienced a lot, you know more than I do; think seriously and tell me: what am I to do? Teach me. If you no longer have the strength to go yourself and take others with you, then at least show me where I should go. You must agree, after all, that I'm a living, feeling and rational person. To find myself in a false position, to play some absurd role… that's hard for me. I'm not reproaching you, I'm not blaming you, I'm just asking.'

Tea was brought.

'Well then?' asked Zinaida Fyodorovna, passing me a glass. 'What can you tell me?'

'There are other fish in the sea,' I replied. 'There are other people besides me, Zinaida Fyodorovna.'

'Well, point them out to me,' she said animatedly. 'That's all I'm asking of you.'

'And I'd like to say something else too,' I continued. 'It's possible to serve an idea in more than one field. If you're mistaken, if you've lost faith in one thing, you can find something else. The world of ideas is wide and inexhaustible.'

'The world of ideas!' she said and looked me mockingly in the face. 'It'd be better if we stopped… What's the point…'

87

She blushed.

'The world of ideas!' she repeated, throwing her napkin aside, and her face took on an expression of indignation and disgust. 'All these fine ideas of yours, I can see, come down to one inevitable, essential step: I must become your lover. That's what's needed. To make much of ideas without being the lover of the most honest, the most ideological man means not to understand the ideas. You should start from there... from the lover, that is, and everything else will take care of itself.'

'You're irritable, Zinaida Fyodorovna,' I said.

'No, I'm honest!' she shouted, breathing hard. 'I'm honest.'

'Perhaps you are honest, but you're mistaken, and it hurts me to listen to you.'

'I'm mistaken!' she laughed. 'You're the last person to be talking of that, my good sir. I may seem indelicate, cruel to you, but so be it: do you love me? You do love me, don't you?'

I shrugged my shoulders.

'Yes, you shrug your shoulders!' she continued sarcastically. 'When you were ill and delirious I heard you, then all the time these adoring eyes, sighs, well-meaning conversations about intimacy, spiritual kinship... But most important, why have you been dishonest right up until now? Why have you concealed what is, while talking about what is not? If you'd said right from the start which ideas in particular made you drag me away from St Petersburg, then at least I would have known. I would have poisoned myself then as I intended, and there wouldn't be this tedious comedy now... Oh, what's the point of talking!' She waved a hand at me in exasperation and sat down.

'You speak in a tone that suggests you suspect me of dishonourable intentions,' I said, offended.

'Oh, come on. What do you mean? It's not intentions I suspect in you, but rather that you had no intentions. If you had had them, I would have known them. Apart from ideas and love you didn't have anything. Ideas and love now, and in prospect – I become your lover. That's the order of things, both in life and in novels... You criticised him,' she said, striking the table with the palm of her hand, 'yet in the end, like it or not, you agree with him. It's not for nothing he despises all these ideas.'

'He doesn't despise ideas, he's afraid of them,' I shouted. 'He's a coward and a liar.'

'Oh, come on! He's a coward, a liar, and he deceived me, but what about you? Excuse my being frank: who are you? He deceived me and abandoned me to my fate in St Petersburg, and you've deceived me and abandoned me here. But at least he didn't drag ideas into his deceit, whereas you...'

'For God's sake, why are you saying this?' I said in horror, wringing my hands and rushing up to her. 'No, Zinaida Fyodorovna, no, this is cynicism, you mustn't despair like this, hear me out,' I continued, seizing on a thought which suddenly flashed indistinctly through my mind and which, it seemed, might yet save us both. 'Listen to me. I've experienced a lot in my time, so much that now, when I think back, my head spins, and now I understand fully with my brain and with my tormented soul that a man either has no purpose, or else it lies in just one thing – selfless love for his neighbour. That is where we should go and where our purpose lies! That is my faith!'

I wanted to say some more about mercy and exoneration, but my voice suddenly sounded insincere and I became embarrassed.

'I want to live!' I said sincerely. 'To live and live! I want peace and quiet, I want warmth, this sea, to have you near. Oh, how I'd love to instil in you too this passionate thirst for life! You've just been talking of love, but it would be enough for me simply to have you near, your voice, your expression…'

She blushed and said rapidly to prevent me from speaking, 'You love life, but I hate it. So we have differing paths.'

She poured herself some tea, but did not touch it, went into the bedroom and lay down.

'I suggest it would be better for us to stop this conversation,' she said to me from there. 'Everything is already over for me, and I don't need anything… There's no use in carrying on talking!'

'No, everything's not over!'

'Oh, come on!… I know! I'm sick of it… That's enough.'

I stood for a while, walked from one corner to the other and went out into the corridor. Later on, when I went up to her door late in the night and listened, I distinctly heard crying.

The next morning the hotel footman, while handing me my clothes, informed me with a smile that the lady from room thirteen was giving birth. I dressed as best I could and, with my heart stopping in horror, I hurried to Zinaida Fyodorovna. In her room were the doctor, a midwife and an elderly Russian lady from Kharkov by the name of Darya Mikhailovna. There was a smell of ether. I had scarcely crossed the threshold when from the room where she lay there came a quiet, mournful groan, and, as if the wind had carried it to me from Russia, I remembered Orlov, his irony, Polya, the Neva, flakes of snow, then the cab without an apron, the prophecy I read in the cold morning sky and the despairing cry, 'Nina! Nina!'

'Go and see her,' said the lady.

I went in to Zinaida Fyodorovna feeling as though I were the father of the child. She lay with her eyes closed, thin and pale in a white lacy bonnet. I recall there were two expressions on her face: one indifferent, cold, listless; the other, which was lent her by the white bonnet, childlike and helpless. She did not hear me come in, or perhaps heard, yet paid no attention to me. I stood watching her and waited.

But then her face contorted in pain, she opened her eyes and began to gaze at the ceiling, as if trying to understand what was the matter with her... Her face expressed repugnance.

'It's vile,' she whispered.

'Zinaida Fyodorovna,' I called weakly.

She looked at me listlessly, with indifference, and closed her eyes. I stood for a while and then left.

During the night Darya Mikhailovna informed me that a baby girl had been born, but that the mother's condition was serious; later people were running down the corridor and there was some noise. Darya Mikhailovna came to me once more and with despair on her face, wringing her hands, she said, 'Oh, it's awful! The doctor suspects she took poison! Oh, how badly Russians behave themselves here!'

The next day at noon Zinaida Fyodorovna passed away.

18

Two years went by. Circumstances changed, I came back to St Petersburg and could now live here without hiding. I was no longer afraid of being and seeming sensitive and committed myself fully to the paternal or, to be more accurate, idolatrous feeling aroused in me by Sonya, Zinaida Fyodorovna's daughter. I fed her from my own hands, bathed and put her to bed, did not take my eyes off her for whole nights at a time and cried out when I thought the nurse was about to drop her. My thirst for the ordinary life of an ordinary person became with the passage of time ever stronger and more impatient, but my wide-ranging dreams stopped in the vicinity of Sonya, as if they had finally found in her the very thing I needed. I loved this little girl madly. In her I saw the continuation of my own life, and I did not merely think, but felt, almost believed that when I finally cast off my long, bony, bearded body, I would live on in these little blue eyes, the silky blond hair and these tiny, plump, pink hands which stroked my face and hugged my neck so lovingly.

Sonya's fate frightened me. Her father was Orlov, her name on her birth certificate was Krasnovskaya, and the only person to know of and take an interest in her existence, that is I, was already nearing the end of his song. It needed to be given serious thought.

The day after my arrival in St Petersburg I set off to visit Orlov. The door was opened to me by a fat old man with ginger sideburns and no moustache, evidently a German. Polya, who was tidying the sitting-room, did not recognise me, but Orlov, on the other hand, recognised me immediately.

'Ah, the gentleman plotter!' he said, looking me over curiously and laughing. 'What brings you here?'

He had not changed at all: still the same sleek, unpleasant face, the same irony. And on the table, as in previous times, there lay some new book with an ivory knife marking a page. He had obviously been reading before my arrival. He sat me down, offered me a cigar and, with a delicacy characteristic only of people who have been extremely well brought up, concealing the unpleasant feeling aroused in him by my face and my emaciated figure, he remarked in passing that I had not changed at all and was easily recognised, even though I now had quite a growth of beard. We talked about the weather, about Paris. In order to get the inevitable, difficult question tormenting both him and me over with quickly, he asked, 'Is Zinaida Fyodorovna dead?'

'Yes, she died.'

'In childbirth?'

'Yes, in childbirth. The doctor suspected a different cause of death, but... both for you and for me it's less disturbing to think that she died in childbirth.'

He gave a sigh for the sake of propriety and fell silent. All was quiet for a moment.

'Well then. Everything's as it used to be here, no particular changes,' he began animatedly, noticing that I was examining the study. 'My father, as you know, left office and is retired now, I'm still in the same place. Do you remember Pekarsky? He's still the same. Gruzin died last year of diphtheria... Well, and Kukushkin is alive and often reminisces about you. Incidentally,' continued Orlov, lowering his eyes shyly, 'when Kukushkin found out who you were, he began claiming to people everywhere that you'd committed an assault on him, had meant to kill him... and that he'd barely survived.'

I remained silent.

'Old servants don't forget their masters... It's very nice on your part,' joked Orlov. 'However, would you like some wine or coffee? I'll order some to be brewed.'

'No, thank you. I've come to see you on a very important matter, Georgy Ivanych.'

'I'm not a lover of important matters, but I'm glad to be of assistance. What can I do for you?'

'You see,' I began anxiously, 'I have here with me now the late Zinaida Fyodorovna's daughter… I've looked after her upbringing until now, but as you can see, I could become nothing more than a name any day. I should like to die with the idea that she is settled.'

Orlov blushed slightly, frowned and threw me a fleeting stern glance. It was not so much the 'important matter' that had had an unpleasant effect on him as my words about becoming a mere name, about death.

'Yes, it needs to be given thought,' he said, shielding his eyes as if from the sun. 'I'm grateful to you. You say it's a little girl?'

'Yes, a little girl. A wonderful little girl.'

'Right. Of course, this isn't a pet dog, but a person… clearly it needs to be given serious thought. I'm prepared to take part and… and I'm much obliged to you.'

He got up and walked around, biting his fingernails, then stopped in front of a picture.

'This needs to be given thought,' he said in a muffled voice, standing with his back to me. 'I shall see Pekarsky today and ask him to pay a visit to Krasnovsky. I don't expect Krasnovsky will be difficult for long and I'm sure he'll agree to take the little girl.'

'But, forgive me, I don't know what Krasnovsky has to do with it,' I said, rising as well and going up to a picture at the other end of the room.

'But after all, she does bear his name, I hope!' said Orlov.

'Yes, he is perhaps obliged by law to take the child in. I don't know, but I didn't come to you, Georgy Ivanych, to talk about laws.'

'No, no, you're right,' he agreed rapidly. 'I seem to be

talking nonsense. But don't you worry. We'll discuss all this to our mutual satisfaction. If not one thing, then the other, if not that, then something else, but one way or another this ticklish question will be resolved. Pekarsky will arrange everything. Be so good as to leave me your address and I shall inform you immediately of the decision we reach. Where are you staying?'

Orlov made a note of my address, sighed and said with a smile:

'What a commission, though, dear Lord,
To be a baby daughter's dad![9]

'But Pekarsky will arrange everything. He has his head screwed on. Did you stay long in Paris?'

'A month or two.'

We were silent. Orlov was obviously afraid that I would begin to talk about the girl again, and to draw my attention in another direction he said, 'You've probably already forgotten about your letter. But I kept it. I understand your mood at that time and, I confess, I respect that letter. "Damned cold blood", "an Asiatic", "braying laughter" – it's all nice and full of character,' he continued with an ironic smile. 'And the basic idea is possibly close to the truth, although one could argue about it endlessly. Not about the idea itself, that is,' he faltered, 'but with your attitude to the question, with your temperament, so to speak. Yes, my life is abnormal, spoilt, no good for anything, and I am prevented from starting a new life by cowardice – you are absolutely right there. But the fact that you take it to heart so, are anxious and fall into despair – that isn't reason, there you are completely wrong.'

'A living man cannot fail to be anxious and despairing when he sees how he is perishing himself and how others are perishing around him.'

'Absolutely! I'm not preaching indifference by any means, I just want an objective attitude to life. The more objective, the less risk of falling into error. You need to look into the root and seek in everything the cause of all causes. We've grown weak, sunk, in the end fallen, our generation consists entirely of neurasthenics and whiners, all we can do is talk about weariness and exhaustion, but it's not you or I that is to blame for this: we're too small for the fate of a whole generation to depend on our will. Here, one must assume, there are major, common causes which, from a biological point of view, have their own sound *raison d'être*. We are neurasthenic, miserable, recreant, but maybe that is necessary and helpful for the generations which will live after us. Not a single hair falls from a head without the will of our Heavenly Father – in other words, in nature and in the human environment nothing is done without reason. All is well-founded and essential. And if that is so, then why should we be particularly worried and write despairing letters?'

'That's as may be,' I said after some thought. 'I believe that subsequent generations will find things easier and clearer; our experience will be at their service. But after all, one would like to live irrespective of future generations and not only on their behalf. Life is given once, and one would like to live it cheerfully, sensibly and beautifully. One would like to play a conspicuous, independent, noble role, to make history so that those same generations did not have the right to say of each of us, "that was a nonentity", or something still worse... I too believe in the expediency and the necessity of what happens around us, but what has that necessity to do with me, why should my *I* be lost?'

'Well, what can be done!' sighed Orlov and stood up, as if

letting me know that our conversation was now over.

I took hold of my hat.

'We've been sitting for just half an hour, but to think how many questions we've solved!' said Orlov, seeing me out into the hall. 'So I'll take care of the... I'll see Pekarsky this very day. Don't give it a second thought.'

He stopped and waited for me to put my things on, evidently feeling pleasure at the fact that I was about to go.

'Georgy Ivanych, give me back my letter,' I said.

'Yes sir!'

He went into the study and returned a minute later with the letter. I thanked him and left.

The next day I received a note from him. He congratulated me on the successful resolution of the question. There was a lady of Pekarsky's acquaintance, he wrote, who kept a boarding-house, a nursery of sorts, where they accepted even very small children. The lady could be relied upon completely, but before coming to an agreement with her, it would do no harm to discuss things with Krasnovsky – formality demanded it. He advised me to go to see Pekarsky straight away and at the same time to take with me the birth certificate, if there was one. 'Accept my assurance of the sincere respect and devotion of your humble servant...'

I read this letter while Sonya sat on the table watching me carefully, unblinking, as though she knew that her fate was being decided.

NOTES

1. Orlov is generally referred to in the formal manner by his given name (pronounced with two hard 'g's, as in the word 'go') and patronymic, but also in the French manner as 'Georges' and, occasionally, with the use of an affectionate diminutive 'Georgey'.

2. Kozma Prutkov was the pseudonym used by A.K. Tolstoy and the brothers Zhemchuzhnikov for publication of their comic and satirical writings between the 1850s and 1880s.

3. 'What does the coming day hold for me?' This aria is sung on the eve of his death in a duel by the young Romantic poet Lensky in Tchaikovsky's operatic version of Pushkin's novel in verse, *Eugene Onegin* (1823).

4. 'Come secretly thinking of me' is a line from an Italian song used in the epigraph to Turgenev's short story, 'Three Meetings', as well as in the body of the text.

5. The hero of Turgenev's novel *On the Eve* (1859) is committed to the liberation of his native Bulgaria from Ottoman control, an objective shared by the Russian woman who loves him.

6. In its Russian translation, Hamlet's line to Ophelia in Shakespeare's *Hamlet* ('Get thee to a nunnery') is slightly adapted by Gruzin, who uses the polite plural form of 'you' when speaking to Zinaida Fyodorovna.

7. The novel of 1861, *The Humiliated and Insulted*.

8. The drama, *Les Pauvres de Paris*, by Edouard Brisebarre and Eugène Nus was performed in a Russian version in the 1870s in Taganrog, where it was presumably seen by Chekhov.

9. Orlov quotes two lines of Alexander Griboyedov's 1820s verse comedy 'Grief from Wit', many phrases from which are still used in Russian even today, but substitutes the word 'baby' for the original 'grown-up'.

BIOGRAPHICAL NOTE

Anton Pavlovich Chekhov was born in Taganrog, Russia, in January 1860. The son of a grocer, he studied medicine in Moscow, where he began writing short stories and comic sketches. He also wrote often humorous one-act dramas, although it is for his later, more serious plays that he is celebrated. He began practising medicine in 1884, and in 1887 his first full-length play, *Ivanov* was produced in St Petersburg. In 1888 he won the Pushkin Prize for 'The Steppe', a short story in his third published collection. A keen humanitarian, Chekhov worked in a free clinic for peasants, assisting in famine and epidemic relief. After a disastrous first production of *The Seagull* in St Petersburg in 1895, Chekhov vowed never to write for the theatre again, but the Moscow Arts Theatre production of 1897 was a success, as was *Uncle Vanya* in 1899. *Three Sisters* (1901) and *The Cherry Orchard* (1904) followed.

In 1897, Chekhov discovered that he suffered from consumption, and thereafter lived in the Crimea, travelling to Moscow only to advise on his productions. In 1901 he married the actress Olga Knipper who played a number of his characters on stage. Chekhov's vastly innovative and influential prose and drama focus on what Maxim Gorky termed 'the tragedy of life's trivialities' – the unhappy and banal lifestyles of his Russian contemporaries. He died in July 1904 and was buried in Moscow.

Hugh Aplin studied Russian at the University of East Anglia and Voronezh State University, and worked at the University of Leeds and St Andrews before taking up his current post as Head of Russian at Westminster School, London.

HESPERUS PRESS – 100 PAGES

Hesperus Press, as suggested by the Latin motto, is committed to bringing near what is far – far both in space and time. Works written by the greatest authors, and unjustly neglected or simply little known in the English-speaking world, are made accessible through new translations and a completely fresh editorial approach. Through these short classic works, each little more than 100 pages in length, the reader will be introduced to the greatest writers from all times and all cultures.

For more information on Hesperus Press, please visit our website: **www.hesperuspress.com**

To place an order, please contact:
Grantham Book Services
Isaac Newton Way
Alma Park Industrial Estate
Grantham
Lincolnshire NG31 9SD
Tel: +44 (0) 1476 541080
Fax: +44 (0) 1476 541061
Email: orders@gbs.tbs-ltd.co.uk

SELECTED TITLES FROM HESPERUS PRESS

Gustave Flaubert *Memoirs of a Madman*

Alexander Pope *Scriblerus*

Ugo Foscolo *Last Letters of Jacopo Ortis*

Joseph von Eichendorff *Life of a Good-for-nothing*

Mark Twain *The Diary of Adam and Eve*

Giovanni Boccaccio *Life of Dante*

Victor Hugo *The Last Day of a Condemned Man*

Joseph Conrad *Heart of Darkness*

Edgar Allan Poe *Eureka*

Emile Zola *For a Night of Love*

Daniel Defoe *The King of Pirates*

Giacomo Leopardi *Thoughts*

Nikolai Gogol *The Squabble*

Franz Kafka *Metamorphosis*

Herman Melville *The Enchanted Isles*

Leonardo da Vinci *Prophecies*

Charles Baudelaire *On Wine and Hashish*

William Makepeace Thackeray *Rebecca and Rowena*

Wilkie Collins *Who Killed Zebedee?*

Théophile Gautier *The Jinx*

Charles Dickens *The Haunted House*

Luigi Pirandello *Loveless Love*

Fyodor Dostoevsky *Poor People*

E.T.A. Hoffmann *Mademoiselle de Scudéri*

Henry James *In the Cage*

Francesco Petrarch *My Secret Book*

D.H. Lawrence *The Fox*

Percy Bysshe Shelley *Zastrozzi*